TRAPPED BY COAL

Constance Horne

Illustrations by Linda Heslop

MYLA

Pacific Educational Press
Vancouver Canada

Published by Pacific Educational Press
Faculty of Education
University of British Columbia
Vancouver B.C. V6T 1Z4
Telephone: (604) 822-5385
Fax: (604) 822-6603

The publisher would like to thank Canadian Heritage and
the Canada Council for their support of its publishing pro-
gram. The publisher would also like to thank Sarah Heslop,
Erica Drew, and Jeffrey Drew of Victoria, B.C. for acting as
models for the illustrator.

Canadian Cataloguing in Publication Data
Horne, Constance
  Trapped by coal

  ISBN 0-88865-091-4

  I. Heslop, Linda. II. Title.
PS8565.06693T72 1994   jC813'.54   C94-91064503
PZ7.H67Tr 1994

Illustrations: Linda Heslop
Design: Warren Clark
Printed in Canada

10   9   8   7   6   5   4   3   2

Contents

Chapter One

*M*illie was clearing the table after her brother's dinner. The last thing she picked up was a plate of jam tarts. Art hadn't eaten any. She glanced at him as he stood at the window of the front room looking through the lace curtains to the snow outside. She knew he was too nervous to eat. They had all been on edge since Art came in from work at 3:30 and told Mum that the mine manager was coming to visit them in about an hour.

For a moment Mum had frozen, then she'd said calmly, "So, it's come. Wash up and eat your dinner. At least we'll know the worst."

Ben pulled at Millie's sleeve. "Can I have a tart?" he asked.

Millie held the plate down to her little brother. Let him eat while he could.

"Don't cram it in!" she scolded. "And one's enough."

She was interrupted by Art. "Mr. Warbell's here," he called.

Mum came into the kitchen from the washroom where she had been cleaning up after Art's scrubbing. As she spoke, she removed her apron and hung it behind the door.

"Millie, you take Ben and go to the Gauthiers'. Hurry now. Into your coats and away you go." She shooed them into the scullery. "Make sure he wears his hat," she called through the closed door, "and wipe his jammy face."

Ben began to say that he wanted to stay home, but Millie's wet rag stopped him. He was getting used to being sent to the neighbour's house. Since their father had been killed in the mine a month ago, he had spent a lot of time there. When he was dressed, Millie grabbed her own coat and did not even bother to button it. She was coming back, no matter what Mum said!

She heard Art greeting Mr. Warbell at the front door as she pushed Ben out the back. Fresh snow had fallen during the night, but by this time of day it was covered with a layer of coal dust. Everything in Extension was always covered with coal dust. It went with the constant clatter of machinery from the busy mine and the sulphury smell from the ever-smouldering slag pile. Without coal the town wouldn't exist, and coal meant dust and dirt. Having lived there all her eleven years, Millie hardly noticed it. It was just part of home. But where would home be after today?

Millie slogged through drifts in two back yards with Ben following in her footsteps. At the third house, Lisette Gauthier and two of her younger brothers were clearing the path to the outhouse. Millie thrust Ben at her friend.

"The manager just arrived at our house. Can you keep Ben for a bit?"

"Yes, but—"

"I don't have time to talk. Send Ben home when you see the manager leave, all right?"

Lisette nodded.

Millie raced back to the house and slipped in quietly. Good! The curtain had been drawn across the arch between the kitchen and the front room. From the sewing machine chair she could hear everything without being seen. Mr. Warbell was talking. He must be on the settee. Mum would be in her rocking chair on the other side of the curtain. Better not make a sound! Art coughed. He was at the far end of the room, probably sitting on the chair next to the gramophone.

They must have been talking about Dad. Millie heard Mum say, "Yes, he was a good man."

There was a pause and then Mr. Warbell cleared his throat.

"Well, you know why I'm here, Mrs. Piggott. These houses belong to the Company. With your husband gone..."

"Art works for the mine," Mum interrupted.

"But not underground," answered Mr. Warbell.

In hard times many boys from miners' families quit school and went to work for the company as soon as they turned twelve years old. They helped care for the mules, filled the lamps, sorted coal, or did other jobs on the surface until they were old enough to go down into the mine.

"How long have you been on the picking table, Art?" asked Mr. Warbell.

"Two years, sir," answered Art with a squeak. He coughed and began again in a normal voice. "Almost two years. Since Dad went back to work."

"That was after the strike." The manager's

voice had an edge to it. "Let's see, August, 1914 to February, 1916. That's a year and seven months. Now you know these houses are all rented to men who work underground. That's the colliery rule."

Millie put her feet on the top rung of the chair, wrapped her arms tightly around her legs, and rested her cheek against her knees. This was the moment they had all been dreading. If they were put out of the house, where would they go?

"Mr. Warbell," Mum said. "We have no money. We used up all our savings in the two years the men were on strike."

The man snorted. "Waste of time!" he muttered. "They gained nothing!"

"Nothing but debts," agreed Mum. "It's taken two years of work to pay ours off. We'd only just got on our feet again when Wilf died in your unsafe mine."

"That's not proven!" said Mr. Warbell firmly. "It's likely the rock fell because he hadn't timbered properly."

"You knew Wilf better than that!"

Millie could imagine Mum's tight-lipped look. Surely she wouldn't quarrel with the mine manager just now. After a moment of silence, she spoke calmly. "The thing is, if you put us out, the children will have no roof over their heads. Can't you give us a bit of time? I'll find a job. I used to be a dressmaker in England, but it will take me time to find a position."

"And how will you pay rent? I've been talking to Harold Winlaw at the Fraternal Order. He tells me they've not a cent to offer you."

"They paid for the funeral," said Art.

"Good on them. But that fund's another casualty of the strike. You'll get nothing from them. So how will you pay the rent?"

"I'll get some work," said Mum, "and, with Art's wages, we'll manage."

Millie straightened out and risked a brief peek past the edge of the curtain. Mr. Warbell was shaking his head.

"These houses are for miners," he repeated. "But I do have a proposition for you. You can stay, and we'll even give you six months at half-rent, if young Art goes underground."

From her hiding place, Millie hears the mine manager demand that Art go to work in the mine.

Millie gasped aloud. Luckily, the noise was covered by Mum's own cry of "No!"

"He's only thirteen years old," she went on more calmly.

"I'll be fourteen in a month," said Art.

Mr. Warbell said, "The Inspector of Mines has just been here. By the time he comes again the boy will be of age. Anyway, with the war on, the government wants us to get out all the coal we can. With men joining up, we're short handed. Starting Monday, we've got an opening for a winch boy. Young Shepherd—do you know him, Art?"

"Yes."

"He's getting promoted to rope rider. If you want his job, it's yours."

"His father did not want him in the mine," protested Mum.

Millie heard the man stand up.

"Well, there it is, Mrs. Piggott. If your son goes underground, you can stay. Otherwise, you'll have to leave this house."

Millie couldn't understand the long pause. Of course, Mum would say no. Art had weak lungs. The doctor had warned them that he must never work in a mine. Even the dust made by separating rocks from the coal on the picking table was bad for him. Going underground would kill him. He'd die of black lung disease, just like Granddad, only much sooner.

"I'll take it," she heard Art say. "Thank you, Mr. Warbell."

"Good man! Come and see me at the office tomorrow and we'll give you your disk. Good day, Mrs. Piggott."

"Good day, Mr. Warbell."

Millie waited until the front door clicked shut, then dashed the curtain aside. Mum was rocking fast. Her hands were folded in her lap, and her eyes stared into space. It was so strange to see her sitting idle that for a moment Millie couldn't speak. Art came back in from the hall.

"You can't go into the mine!" she shouted. "Dad said you'd never go underground!"

"You heard the man," answered her brother wearily. He dropped into one corner of the settee. "It's me underground or all of us out in the cold."

"We could move back to the old house," Millie said.

"No, we couldn't. The Company bought all that property from Farmer Ogden at the beginning of the war. That's why we moved here. You know that," he added scornfully. "Anyway, those houses have been condemned. The seam was mined too close to the surface. They'll all fall into the shaft some day."

"Then how come Bart Menzies lives there?"

"Because Mr. Ogden still owns some land on the mountain. He let him build a shack in the woods."

"We could build a shack in the woods."

Mum interrupted. "Millie, leave your brother alone. He's tired. We have to stay in this house, and that's all there is to it."

"He could be killed like Dad!" Millie turned to Effie with blazing eyes. "If you were our real mother, you wouldn't let him go in the mine!"

Effie stopped rocking. Her face flushed. "Oh, so now I'm the wicked stepmother, am I?" she said angrily.

"Shut up, Millie!" Art ordered.

The back door slammed.

"Mummy?" called Ben.

"In here, son." Effie's voice was nearly normal.

Millie's knees gave way. She plopped onto the other end of the settee as Ben ran into the room. He gazed into his mother's face while she took off his snowy hat and coat.

"What's wrong, Mummy? Are you mad at me?"

"Not at you, Ben." She patted her lap and he climbed up. She pulled her skirt out of the way of his wet boots and brushed a lock of damp hair off his forehead. As she watched them, the trembling in Millie's arms and legs got worse. She felt cold all over. What had she said?

"Are we going to move, Mummy?" asked the little boy fearfully.

"Not right away."

"Good." He sighed and snuggled against her.

"Millie, you apologize to Mum," growled Art.

Millie clasped her arms tight against her chest. "I'm sorry," she whispered.

Mum sighed. "The coal's been hard on all of us. The coal killed your Granddad, and there's no doubt but that your mother died of overwork. And now the coal has killed your Dad." She bent her head over Ben's brown curls.

"None of them wanted Art to go into the mine," said Millie stubbornly. "Mummy and Granddad saved money so he wouldn't have to."

"You're making that up!" said Art. "You were only four when Granddad died. You can't remember."

"I do so remember! Granddad had a tin tobacco box. He and Mummy put money in it." In her imagination, Millie could see her mother's hand lifting the lid of the square tin while Granddad's hand held out a coin. "It was to keep you out of the mine."

Mum shook her head at Art to stop the argument. "Well, it's gone now, with the rest of your Dad's savings," she said. "Millie, girl, I know well what your father wanted. But he's not here, is he? And we four have to carry on. Or do you want to change your mind about going to live with your aunt in Nanaimo? She'd gladly take you."

Millie hung her head and did not answer. They'd been over that before. She would never, ever, leave her family.

Mum began to rock gently. "Half a loaf is better than no bread," she said. "We've got six months to get on our feet. That will be the end of August. Art will come to no permanent harm in that time. If we all do our part, we could move to Ladysmith in time for school re-opening, and Art could go back to school."

The black cloud of fear and anger lifted a little from Millie's soul.

"Can we do it?" she asked.

"We can try," said Mum. "But there's no work for me in this little town. I'll have to go into Ladysmith some days. That means you'll have to take over here. It will be extra work for you—a lot of extra work."

"I don't mind!" cried Millie. She sat up straight and squared her shoulders. She felt ready to take on the whole world to save her brother. "I'll do anything!"

"Me, too," Ben piped up. "What can I do?"

His mother laughed and rumpled his hair. "That's my brave wee man." She looked gravely at her two stepchildren. "We've got a goal, then. To have Art out of the mine by the end of August."

"Some hope!" muttered the boy.

Millie reached out and punched him on the arm. "Don't be a spoilsport! We can do it!"

"That's enough, Millie!" said Mum firmly. "Art, I'm sorry about this. It's the best we can do for now. We'll get you out of that mine as soon as we can."

"We sure will!" Millie declared.

Chapter Two

The sun had not yet risen above the mountain when Art arrived at the lamphouse on Monday morning. The room was crowded with miners who had come on the train from Ladysmith where most of them lived. They were waiting to exchange their identification disks for headlamps. Art knew very few of them. When he joined the line, the man in front of him turned around and grinned.

"Who's this, then?" he asked loudly. "New man on the job?"

Other men turned to look. Art knew that the miners always played tricks on newcomers, especially boys in their first few days underground. He tried to grin bravely. A hand dropped onto his shoulder and he looked up into the face of Pete Gauthier, their neighbour.

"Yeah, his first day underground," said

Pete. "This here is Art Piggott. He's Wilf's son."

The leer faded from the first man's face. "I knew yer Dad. Good mate, he was."

Others nodded and turned away. Art let out his breath. Maybe they would leave him alone, at least for today.

When his turn came, he took the lighted lamp and clipped it to his hat while the lampman hung the disk on the hook under the date and time of the shift: March 1, 1916, 8 a.m. If a disaster happened, the rescue team would know who was down below. Just a month ago, the mine whistle had blown three times to call them to the rock fall in which Art's father had died. One blast of the whistle marked the beginning and end of every shift. Two blasts called the doctor. When an evacuation of the whole mine was necessary, the whistle tooted six or seven times. Art hoped he would never hear that signal.

Because Extension was a level entry mine, the outside light made the lamps unnecessary for the first few meters beyond the entrance. Art saw Dick Shepherd waiting for him. He stood astride a narrow ditch through which water poured out of the mine. He was out of the way of the stream of men and mules walking on the pathway alongside the double railway tracks. Most of the miners were riding in the empty coal cars being hauled in by a small locomotive.

"I'm to show you your job," said Dick and hopped into a car. Art followed him.

The main tunnel was wide and high and well lit by the headlight of the locie and the lamps of the men crowded together. Art had noticed before that the smell of the coal dust which permeated everyone's work clothes was different from the smell of the actual coal. Here, as the train moved slightly upward into the heart of the mine, the sulphur odour of the damp coal became stronger. The men were chattering about the war news or the big Red Cross concert on Saturday night in Ladysmith at which some of them had performed.

About two kilometers in, at Level One, the train stopped to drop off several cars and many of the men's tin lunch pails clattered, adding a high note to the rumble and screech of the metal wheels being shunted to another track. After another kilometer and a half, Dick poked Art.

"This is us," he said. "Level Two."

With the other men, they began the long walk past stalls where coal had already been mined. This tunnel was much narrower and lower than the main one. There was just enough room for the double track of rail lines which shone when light from the lamps hit them. As they climbed up between the rails, Art could hear the jingle of harness and the snorts of mules behind him. The mine was carved out of the mountain and the main tunnel had been driven in at a slight upward slope to provide drainage. On Level Two, the coal seam took a sharp downward turn. Mules could not pull the loaded cars, weighing about a ton each, up the slope. An electric winch had been installed, and here Art was to work.

As the men and mules tramped past, Dick showed him two levers. One started the motor that drove the pulleys around which the continuous rope wound as it pulled the cars on the rails. The other lever threw a switch on the track so that he could stop a car if necessary.

"When I've hooked up four or five cars down below," said Dick. "I'll signal you on this bell here." He reached up and pulled the cord on a small brass bell. Tink, tink, tink. "Three rings and you start the motor. See?"

Art nodded.

"That pulls the load up and because it's a

loop the empties come up from the main tunnel at the same time. See?"

"Yes."

"Right. I'll be riding rope to unhook them so the locie can haul them out. So I'll see you every trip. Tell you what, I'll leave my lunch pail here with you and we'll eat together. That way, you can ask me anything I forgot. Suit you?"

"Yes."

He ran down into the blackness and Art was left with only the feeble light of his headlamp. He was utterly alone with solid blackness walling him in on three sides. If he gazed hard enough back the way they had come, he could see a faint glimmer of light. It was like the beginning of dawn on the horizon outside. Of course, there the sun rose and gradually the light spread over the whole town. Down here, the pale line never changed. Would he ever get used to the darkness?

He shuddered. It was so lonely here. Up at the tipple, he had had his partner Lee to talk to. While they sorted coal from rock, they could see many workers: dumpers, other pickers, train drivers and loaders, and over at the stables, the boys who cared for the mules. There was one good thing about being below, though. He was out of the weather. On a wet day like today, wind and rain would be blowing in through the open sides of the picking table shed.

He listened. At the winch he was too far from the face to hear the miners' picks and shovels, and this early in the shift no cars were moving. The loudest sound was the whirr of the huge ventilator fans which swept deadly methane gas out of the mine. He could also hear water trickling down the walls and rats scurrying around. They were probably picking up crumbs from the lunch of the winch boy on the last shift. That scraping noise might be rock shifting over his head. It was falling rock that had killed his Dad away off there in the darkness. For a moment fierce anger made his whole body shake. He shouldn't be here! Dad always said no son of his would spend his life underground. But it looked as if that was the way it was going to be. By the time he and Mum earned enough money to escape, he'd be an old man.

Tink, tink, tink!

Ah, his first load.

Carefully, he pushed the lever. The rumble of the cars grew louder and louder and finally he saw a glimmer from a headlamp down

below. At the same time, he got a strong whiff of mule, overpowering the smell of the newly mined coal. He also heard a human voice, but it wasn't Dick's. The words were English, but the intonation was Chinese.

At last, the first car came into view. A dead mule with rigid legs lay on its side on top of the load of black lumps. At the sight of its crushed head, Art almost threw up. On the rope between that car and the next rode a Chinese man with a long whip coiled over his shoulder. A steady stream of curses spewed out of his mouth. He must have remembered every swear word he'd ever heard in the mine. When Dick passed, he grinned and pointed to the man ahead.

"Learn some new cuss words, Art?" he called.

Art replied with a sickly smile. He was too shaken to trust his voice.

Fortunately, there were no more hideous surprises during the rest of the long morning. Later, when the other boy joined him for lunch, Art asked him why the mule driver had been so upset.

For the first time, Art is alone in the dark in the depths of the mine.

"He'll be out of a job," Dick explained. "At least down here. You know the men won that rule in the strike—no Chinese underground. It's the only thing they did win," he added bitterly.

"So how come he was allowed?" asked Art.'

Dick laughed. "Because he's the only one who could drive that ornery mule! It was the strongest and fastest one they have. The men wanted the mule working. No mule, no Jim." He opened the lower section of his lunch pail and took a long drink of water.

Art had lived all his life with the miners' prejudice against the Chinese. He himself did not share it. For the last six months, his partner on the picking table had been a young Chinese man. Lee was fast, efficient, and usually cheerful. Art liked him. But he could understand the miners' fear that they would lose their jobs to men who would work for lower wages.

"Will you get his job?" he asked Dick.

"Naw! I've only started riding rope. I'll have to work at this for months. Anyway, I don't want to be a mule driver. Stubborn vicious brutes. Uh–uh! I want to load for my Dad. That's the way to learn to be a miner."

Dick went on talking eagerly about his ambition to work at the face with pick and shovel.

"You'll be a pit boss someday," said Art. It took years of studying and working underground to become the man in charge of all the operations in the mine on one shift, but Dick loved mining enough to do it.

"Maybe," agreed Dick. "Or a shot boss, setting off explosions to loosen the coal. That'd be fun!"

Art had often heard his father say that a shot boss had the most responsible job in the mine. A man had to know all about explosives and their effects before he was allowed to use them. "Isn't it dangerous?" he asked.

"What isn't in a mine?" answered Dick. "My Dad says that every job has its dangers. Fishing, you could drown. Lumbering, a tree might fall on your dome. Mining's no worse than them. You just got to keep your wits about you, my Dad says."

At the end of the shift, as Art plodded wearily homeward, he saw Lee headed for his shack in Chinatown. There was someone else trapped by coal. Because he was Chinese, he'd only be paid about half of what a white man earned, whatever job he worked at. How could he save money to go home to China? Lee would probably never see his family again.

What am I grousing about? thought Art. I have a family and a home and someday I'll get out of the mine. I really will!

Chapter Three

One Sunday afternoon about a month after Art had started to work underground, Millie was walking home from the Presbyterian Church with Ben and Amy. Before the strike, Amy had been Millie's best friend, but now they only walked to Church together on Sundays. The two girls were talking about their Sunday School teacher's new hat. Millie was sure that it was one Mum had trimmed for the millinery shop in Ladysmith.

"Your Mum's smart!" said Amy in admiration. Then, "Ben!" she screamed.

The little boy's rubber boots had sent up a spray of water as he ran past to join the Gauthier family. Lisette and her two younger brothers were spread out in a line among the stumps in the road. They were peering into puddles and prodding the mud with sticks.

"What are they doing here?" asked Millie. "The Catholic Church service should have been over an hour ago."

"They're looking for something."

Amy tagged unwillingly behind as Millie hurried forward.

"What have you lost, Lisette?" Millie asked.

"The dumb cluck dropped the nickel for the collection," Frank answered scornfully.

"Our Pa will kill us if we don't find it," said Jackie.

"We'll help you look!" Ben told his friend.

Lisette frowned at Amy. "We don't want any help from her," she said.

"Yeah!" jeered Frank. "She'd probably keep the nickel if she found it. Scab! Black-leg! Union buster!"

Amy's cheeks flushed. She looked at Millie, who could not meet her eyes. Then she stalked off without a word.

Millie watched her for a moment and then turned to Frank. She felt like swatting him, but she only said, "She's not a miner, so she can't be a scab."

"Well, her Pa was. He worked all through

the strike. He's for the Company, not the miners. And so is her brother."

"Her brother's at the war now," answered Millie.

"Yeah! He wanted to get away from here because everybody hates scabs!"

"How come you were walking with her anyway?" asked Lisette.

Before Millie could answer, Jackie asked, "Are we stopping now?"

"No," answered his sister crossly. "Keep looking!" She used her stick to draw a circle around a tree stump.

"You'll never find it in all that mess," said Millie. "You're just getting your Sunday clothes all dirty for nothing."

"Yeah, Smarty!" jeered Frank. "You're so good at finding stuff. Why don't you look?"

Millie flinched. It was a good thing he didn't know how hard she'd looked for Granddad's box. Over the last month, she had searched every room in the house and looked through every piece of furniture without finding it.

"Where did you drop the nickel?" she asked.

"How do I know," answered Lisette. "I had it at home and I didn't have it at church."

"Was it in your pocket?"

"I've already looked in all my pockets. Anyway, it was in my glove."

"In your glove? Couldn't you feel it?"

Lisette straightened up and put her hands on her hips.

"Are you going to help or not? If you're not, take your little brother away. He's probably trampling it into the mud."

Millie grabbed Ben by the collar and dragged him onto dry ground. She stared at Lisette. Sometimes she wondered why she remained friends with her.

"When did your Dad give you the nickel?" she asked.

"When we were in the front hall ready to leave. I had my gloves on and I put it in there so it wouldn't get lost."

"Hah!" yelled Frank.

Ignoring him, Millie asked, "Did you go straight out the door?"

"Where else would we go?" Lisette asked sarcastically.

"But we didn't," said Frank. "Jackie had his coat buttoned up all wrong so we had to wait till Lisette fixed it."

"Did you button his coat with your gloves on?" asked Millie.

"Can you do up buttons with gloves on?" Lisette demanded.

"No. So, did you?"

"No! I took them off."

"Where did you put them? In your pocket?"

"No," the other girl answered thoughtfully. "I remember picking them up from the hall table."

"The nickel probably fell out," said Millie with a smirk. "I'll bet it's right on the table."

Frank stared at her open-mouthed. Then he flung his stick away and took off like a rabbit. Yelling, the two smaller boys followed.

When Millie and Lisette caught up, Frank was on the front porch waving the nickel in his hand.

"Boy! You sure are good at finding things, Millie," he yelled. "How do you do it?"

"You just have to make a picture in your mind," she answered smugly.

Later that evening, after tea, Millie was sitting in the front room darning a sock from Mum's big mending basket. As usual on a weekend, the basket was filled with holey socks and ripped shirts belonging to some of the single men at the hotel. Since she now went to Ladysmith to work two days a week,

Mum could no longer keep up. Millie had to help. Although she was glad to be earning money, she wished the young men would send their socks before the holes got bigger than the darning egg. Mum could mend a large hole as neatly as a small one. Millie's big darns always turned out lumpy.

While she worked, Millie thought again of what Frank had said about her being good at finding things. She wished it were true. Then she'd be able to remember where Granddad's money was hidden. When she closed her eyes, she could see the square tin tobacco box. She could see her mother's hands holding it and opening the lid. She could see the folded bill Granddad dropped in. But, try as she would, she could not see where they put the box. It must still be in the old house. It certainly wasn't in this one.

The gramophone began to run down. The words of "Keep the Home Fires Burning" slurred and deepened. Art had his nose in a book and didn't seem to notice. Ben was absorbed in playing with his toy soldiers under the table. Millie gladly put down her work and cranked the handle.

Mum glanced at the clock. "Close the gramophone when this song is over Millie," she said. "Bedtime, my sons."

"I'll just finish this chapter," Art answered without looking up.

"Ah, Mum!" growled Ben.

"Yes, Ben, my boy. Bed. Now. Put the soldiers back in their box."

She folded up the shirt she'd been working on and sat rocking while he obeyed her. When he'd finished, he climbed up into her lap.

"Tell me a story," he begged. "Tell me about the time you came to Extension."

"But you've heard it so many times," she said with a laugh.

"We want to hear it again! Don't we, Millie?"

Millie smiled at him. The story always made her sad at first, but what would her life have been like if Aunt Effie hadn't come here?

"Well, then, I'll begin at the beginning, shall I? Back in England?"

Ben sighed happily and snuggled down.

"I was visiting at home in Hartford with Mum and Dad when the letter came from Wilf Piggott. We knew at once it was bad news, for Ann was always the one to write. And bad news it was. Our dear Ann had died. My Dad turned pale under the coal dust while Mum and I cried buckets. We cried for our poor Ann, for Wilf, and for the little boy and girl. Then at the end of the letter, Wilf wrote, 'Do you think Effie would come out and help me with the children? For I don't know what will come to them, else.'

"'No,' I said. 'No! No! No! I've worked hard to escape from a mining town, and I'll never live in one again!'

"Well, your granny talked about the poor motherless children. Mining's a hard life for a man with children, your grandfather said. He needs someone to help him make a house a home. So, by the end of the day, I said I'd go. I went back to my neat, clean little room in the city and packed my trunk and my carry-all and..."

"Dickie Bird!" shouted Ben.

His mother smiled at him. "I'm glad the canary lived long enough for you to know him. He was a great pet. Five years he lived after I rescued him from a life in the mines. They wanted to send him down to detect gas. If he died, they'd know it was unsafe for the men. I knew if I left him behind, that's where he'd end up. So I sewed a waterproof cover for his cage and brought him along. He hated the trip. He didn't sing a note on the ship or the train or at any of the stopping places. Him who'd been such a singer at home! I wondered if I'd done him a favour after all."

"Poor bird!" said Millie.

"Aye, and poor me!" said Mum. "When I stepped off that train in the dead of night in the pouring rain, I thought I'd arrived at the back of beyond. Then your father told me we had a four mile tramp before us to Extension! He hoisted the trunk onto his back and started off into the pitch black. I wanted to murder the man! I'd put on my best hat, thinking that he'd not want to meet such a travel-stained woman. He never even glanced at it! So I took it off, stowed it in the carry all, and pulled up the hood of my cloak. Then off I tramped with the bag in one hand and the canary cage in the other. I could tell where Wilf was only by the splash of his feet on the puddles. Oh, that road! Was it a road? I couldn't tell. There were a thousand holes and stones and stumps and I crashed into every one of them."

"And you got all wet," said Ben.

"Wet! Soaked to the skin I was! After hours of slogging along, I stopped on a bit of dry ground and put down my bag and the cage.

" 'Wilf!' I called.

" 'What is it?' he said.

" 'This is madness,' I said. Oh, I was angry. 'I can't go another step,' I said.

"Well, you know your Dad. Give him a problem and he'd set about solving it.

" 'Right,' he said. He swung the trunk down off his shoulders and turned his bent back to me. 'Climb on,' he said. 'I'll carry you home and then come back for the trunk.'

"Well, can you picture it? Me, the size I am, up on his back with my bag in one hand and Dickie Bird's cage in the other? And what would I hold on with? Tell me that."

Millie knew that Dad had not carried Mum on his back, but every time she heard the story she saw a picture in her mind, just as Mum described it. She and Ben laughed as they always did at that part.

"Aye! Laugh!" said Mum. "I can laugh at it now myself, but I didn't see the fun then. Still, he'd called my bluff. 'Oh, get on with you,' I said. We both picked up our loads and plowed ahead.

"At last, I smelled the damp sulphur and knew we were near the town. Much as I wanted to get in and out of the rain that smell made me sick. Here I was back in a coal town! Oh, I was bitter! And mad. And scared. And bone-weary! I hadn't a civil word for your Dad when he opened the house door for me."

"But Amy's mother was there," Millie said, hugging herself, "and the house was warm, and she'd made a hot meal for you."

"Aye, Mrs. Brand was a good neighbour. In fact, she was a lifesaver. Saved your Dad's life, I mean. For by the time she'd got me into dry things, and hot tea into me, I was no longer mad enough to kill him. After we'd eaten, he took me in to see you two children sleeping in your beds. Poor, forlorn wee things. Like angels you looked."

Art growled and lifted the book to cover his face.

"Some angels!" crowed Ben.

"Well, Dickie Bird thought he'd reached Heaven," his mother continued. "Next day, the sun shone and he sang his little heart out." She sighed. "It was many a long day before I sang again, let me tell you!"

"But you were glad you came when you married Dad and had me, weren't you?" asked Ben.

"I was indeed! My third blessed angel!" She kissed his hair. "Off to bed now."

Art shut his book with a snap and stood up. "The coal trapped you, though. Just like I'm trapped. The coal never lets you go."

"Don't say that!" cried Millie. "Mum got away once. We will again. I'll find Granddad's box."

"Dreamer!" said Art.

"She found the Gauthiers' nickel!" cried Ben.

His brother turned back in the doorway. "The nickel was real," he said. "There never was a box. She dreamed it up."

Mum led Ben after him and Millie was left alone. I did not dream it up, she thought. I'll show him! It must be somewhere in Granddad's house on Odgen Street. But how can I get into it?

Chapter Four

*I*n bed, Millie tried to put their former home out of her mind. She knew that if she fell asleep thinking about it, her nightmare might return. She would think, instead, of moving to Ladysmith. Art would go to school, and his lungs would get better. Where would they live? Not near the coal docks! It was too dusty there! High up the hill in the clean air would be best. Knowing the town fairly well, she imagined herself walking along one of the streets above the railroad station. She chose a house, and walked in to explore the large, airy rooms. While she was planning where the furniture would go, Art started a coughing fit in the loft above the bedroom she shared with Ben.

Immediately, she was back in the little house up against the mountain on the other side of the colliery. So many sad things had happened in that house. There, Granddad's cough had been ever-present. There, her grandfather and her mother had died. But the scariest thing that had happened there, the one that gave her nightmares, had happened during the strike.

From the beginning, the Brand family had lived next door to the Piggotts in the row of look-alike houses. Millie and Amy were babies together. They'd always been best friends. It was Mrs. Brand who had cared for her and Art until Aunt Effie arrived. But when most of the other miners went on strike, Mr. Brand decided to keep on working. Millie hated him for that. It ended her friendship with Amy and almost got his family killed. Remembering that night, she covered her ears with her pillow, but the sounds of angry shouts and breaking glass were in her head. Behind her closed eyes, she again saw torchlight flickering eerily on the bedroom walls. On that evil night, a gang of men and boys had surrounded the Brand house, singing and shouting anti-scab slogans. While she'd huddled with Mum and her brothers in the front room, Dad had gone out to try to stop the rioters. In a few minutes, he'd come back with a bruise on his cheek.

"There's no reasoning with them," he'd said angrily. "They're just a mob."

"What about Mrs. Brand and the child?" Mum had asked anxiously.

"I saw her and the little girl slip out the back door. Go and look for them, Effie. They'd only be scared of a man hunting for them."

Mum had found them crouched in the raspberry patch. She'd brought them in and wrapped them in blankets.

That was the last time Amy had been in Millie's house. The next day soldiers had come and escorted the Brand family to a Company house on a street full of strikebreakers. One of the evicted families had cleaned up the Brands' place and moved in. Because these houses were on property belonging to Farmer Ogden, the Company could not force the strikers to move. There they had stayed for two long, hard years. Finally, the strike ended and Mr. Ogden sold most of his land to the colliery. When Dad went back underground and Art got a job on the picking table, they'd moved to this bigger Company house. And this is where Dad had died.

Art coughed again. He must get out of the mine! She couldn't stand any more tragedies! If only she could remember where Granddad had kept his box. It must be in that little house! She would have to go back and search for it. But she didn't dare go in the dark, and school took up most of the daylight hours. Besides, there were endless chores to do at home with Mum in Ladysmith two days a week.

Monday morning began, as every school day did, with the raising of the Union Jack flag in the schoolyard. Canada belonged to the British Empire, and the British Empire was at war with Germany and her allies. Even those children whose families came from other countries were proud to salute the Canadian flag which flew over the soldiers in battle. Millie shivered as she stood in her place at one corner of the square formed by the twenty-three children and the teacher. Afterwards, it felt good to get inside the little wooden building. John Pawley, the oldest pupil, had come early to light the stove in the middle of the room. Millie could feel its comforting warmth as she stood beside her desk for the Bible reading and the prayer. Miss Gall, who had a brother in the army, had added a new ceremony to Monday mornings—patriotic exercises. For their war effort the children had chosen The Belgian Relief Fund. The Gauthier parents were Belgian and still had relatives in that war-ravaged country. It was Lisette who had suggested supporting the Fund. She collected the offerings every Monday morning and posted the total on the blackboard. Today it amounted to only twelve cents. She thumped down in her seat with a frown on her face. Her place on the platform was taken by a serious little grade three boy. The children stood at attention beside their desks as he read the Honour Roll solemnly.

"Extension men who are serving their King and Country in the Great War."

He intoned the six names.

For some reason she didn't understand, Millie always wanted to giggle when she was supposed to be most serious. Thinking of her Dad made the giggles go away, so she was able to listen quietly as Mickey read.

"Those who have made the Supreme Sacrifice." Mickey recited the names of the three men who had died, including his own uncle. Bowing his head, he led the class in the response, "We will remember them."

Before everyone was seated, Frank Gauthier's hand was waving. "Please, Teacher."

Millie sat right behind him. She knew from his falsely innocent tone that he was going to say something mean. Miss Gall, ready to show each grade its first assignment, paused with her pointer in her hand.

"Yes, Frank?"

He stood up. "Please, Miss Gall, I don't think Adam Brand should be on that list. He's not a soldier, he's just an ambulance driver."

Millie felt as if a pair of cold, giant hands had pinned her to her seat. Only her eyes could move towards Amy who was sitting across the aisle. The girl was rigid, with a fixed, blank look on her face.

When would people like Frank stop persecuting the scabs? thought Millie. The strike had been over for two years! Her Dad had once told her that the men who kept working through the strike were not badly treated in the mine. Down there, where every man's life might depend on his fellow workers, there was no room for grudges. Up above, it was a different story. The strikebreaker and his family were outcasts. It wasn't fair! Amy wasn't a scab! Millie looked at Miss Gall. Although her cheeks were burning, the teacher's voice was icy.

"What does it say here, Frank?" she asked, touching her pointer to the heading above the names on the board.

"Extension men who are serving their King and Country," he read.

"Exactly. Serving," Miss Gall said. "The men of the Medical Corps are serving their fellow soldiers. They are often under fire when they go into the battle to rescue wounded men. Their lives are in danger. We must all pray for the safety of Adam Brand as we do for all soldiers. If he is killed, his name will be added to those who have made the Supreme Sacrifice."

By the time she had finished her speech, the room was perfectly still. Those who had grinned at Frank in agreement turned back to their desks and waited until she said, "Sit down, Frank. Class, your assignments are on the board. Get busy."

With a sigh of relief, Millie turned to look at Amy. The girl was shuddering uncontrollably. Without thinking, Millie stepped across the aisle and slid into the seat beside her. At her touch, Amy dropped her head onto the desk. Millie wrapped an arm around her and laid her cheek on Amy's hair.

"Frank's a stinker," she murmured. "Don't mind him."

A minute later she sensed the teacher standing beside her and felt a light hand on her shoulder.

"Go on with your work now, girls," said a soft voice.

Millie did not get another chance to speak to Amy that morning. At recess, because the ground was still sopping wet, Miss Gall led the children in physical exercises beside their desks. As soon as they were dismissed at noon, Amy ran off home. Millie couldn't catch up to her because she had to fill a water bucket at the school well for Art's after-work bath. Lisette didn't wait for her either.

On the slow walk home she had plenty of time to think about Amy. Why couldn't they be friends again? At Sunday School the two of them read the lesson together, heard one another's memory work, and helped the minister's wife with the little ones. It was a happy time. And yet the rest of the week she acted as though Amy didn't exist. It made no sense!

She set down the bucket to rest her hand.

"Hurry up, Millie!" called Ben from the Gauthiers' front gate. "I'm starving."

At home, they went in the scullery door, and Millie emptied the pail into the copper boiler.

"You get out the bread and butter while I start this fire," she ordered her brother.

Paper and kindling were already laid in the small stove. She lit them and added coal. The water would get hot in the hour she and Ben were home. Before she left, she would bank the fire. The water would still be warm when Art came in after three o'clock. Mum, travelling home on the train that brought the miners for the afternoon shift, would arrive about the same time.

"What are we having on this bread?" called Ben from the kitchen.

"Roast beef," answered Millie. "But don't you try cutting it. I'll do it."

Ben devoured two sandwiches and washed them down with big gulps of milk. Between bites, he gave a long, detailed account of his morning at the Gauthiers'. Millie listened and nodded or grunted at the right places, but her mind was on her own problem. What would happen if she played with Amy? She didn't think Mum or Art would mind. And she was pretty sure Dad wouldn't have cared. He had been on the side of the strikers, and would never have scabbed, but he didn't hate the strikebreakers like some people did. The Gauthiers, for instance. Frank was so mean! As if it wasn't bad enough to know your brother was always in danger! To have people saying mean things about him, too! That must be awful!

Ben reached into the cupboard for the tart tin.

"How many can I have?" he asked.

"One!" said Millie firmly. "Leave some for Art's tea."

"He doesn't like the lemon ones," Ben answered.

"All right, you can have two lemon."

"I don't like lemon all that much either. But I'll take one to use them up." He reachd in with his left hand and then his right. "I'll have another jam one to take away the taste."

Millie grabbed the tin from him and put it away. She tidied the kitchen, set the table for Art's meal, and wiped Ben's hands and face.

By the time she'd finished, she'd made up her mind. On the way back to school, she would tell Lisette that she was going to play with Amy. Maybe she could be friends with them both.

When Lisette came out, she and Frank were deep in an argument that had probably been going on all noon hour. By now it was mostly 'Yes, you did', 'No, I didn't.' There was no chance for Millie to speak.

For the grade sixes' first afternoon lesson, Miss Gall asked them to choose a story and prepare it for a dramatic reading on Friday afternoon. Millie loved dramatic readings. She sang like a crow and was always left out when the Friday performance involved music. But she could read well. The others recognized this and gave her the longest and most important part. She and Lisette had already decided that if they got a chance they would do "The Golden Eagle's Nest." This story of a young woman who miraculously found the strength to climb up a steep cliff and rescue her baby from an eagle's nest was just the sort of sentimental tale they loved. Millie would be the narrator, Lisette would read the mother's words and thoughts, and Amy would play the villagers who waited and watched.

They went out onto the porch to read aloud. It would spoil the performance if the others heard them practicing. As they settled on the steps, Millie smiled because the three of them were doing something together, almost as if they were best friends. Only, if she was a real friend, shouldn't she offer to let Amy be the narrator? She could read very well. She was almost as good as Millie. Well, not really as good. Besides, she was shy and wouldn't want to do it. And if Millie gave up the best role, Lisette would take it, and she always read in the same flat, singsong rhythm. This story needed lots of dramatic pauses and changes in tone. It wouldn't be fair to the audience to let Lisette read it.

By the time they'd been through it once, Millie knew she couldn't possibly give up her part. The story was so sad, so beautiful!

Then she had a really bright idea of how she could be friendly to Amy without making Lisette mad. Amy would be so glad!

"Let's stay after school and practice," she said eagerly.

"I can't," Amy replied. "I have to go home and help my mother."

Well! Couldn't Amy see she was trying to be friends? You'd think she'd jump at the chance!

She followed the other two back to their desks. Amy didn't even look at her as she started on her spelling lesson. Maybe it wasn't going to be so easy making friends again.

Chapter Five

The Friday reading was a success. Millie saw tears on some faces. Even those children who smirked at the sentimentality sat on the edges of their seats in the suspenseful parts.

The reading was fun for all three of them, but it didn't change Lisette's attitude towards Amy. Outside of school, she was the enemy. Was Millie going to have to choose between them? It would be hard to give up Lisette. The Gauthier family had been kind neighbours all through the hard time after Wilf Piggott's death. Ben would hate to lose his friend Jackie. And, if Millie were no longer friends with Lisette but remained friends with Amy, would Mrs. Gauthier still look after Ben when Mum was at work? Not that Amy showed any signs of wanting to be friends except on Sunday mornings. She had to give Lisette and Amy a chance to become friends. But what would Amy and Lisette want to do so much that they'd do it together?

One day in mid-April, Mum came home from Ladysmith with a big smile on her face. Although she had steady work with the milliner one day a week, on the other day she did sewing in people's homes if they needed it. Sometimes, she earned only twenty-five cents. Between them, she and Art managed to pay for only the daily necessities. So far they had saved nothing towards their hoped-for move.

"This is my big chance," Effie told the children at dinner. "The Marshalls are a rich family with lots of friends. Their daughter was going to be married in June, and the whole family ordered new clothes. Now her soldier boyfriend has been called up, and the wedding has been put forward to Easter Monday. Their dressmaker needs help—and they've asked me!"

"Will we get rich, too, Mummy?" asked Ben.

Effie laughed. "Not rich, my son. But think of all the people who'll see my work!"

"They'll all talk about it," said Millie happily. She put her nose in the air and held a teacup with her little finger sticking up. "What a beautiful dress, my dear," she said in a refined English accent. "Who's your dressmaker?"

"A little woman from Extension," answered Art in a falsetto tone.

"Mum's not little!" roared Ben.

"Ah, but she's marrrrvelous, m'dear," Art went on. "You rahlly should try her."

Ben laughed so hard he choked. Mum slapped him on the back.

"All joking aside," she said, "there is a serious side to this. My days will be very long. Sometimes I'll come home with the graveyard shift. Can you manage by yourselves?"

Ben wasn't keen on being put to bed by his big sister, but he said he could stand it for a few days.

On the Friday night before the wedding, Effie brought home a parcel wrapped in an old linen sheet. Before Art went to work on Saturday, he helped her move the sewing machine from the kitchen to her own bedroom. Then she started to undo the string of the parcel.

"This is the dress for the bride's youngest sister," she told Ben and Millie. "I have to finish it today, so you're to stay out of this room. I don't want a speck of dust anywhere near this white material. Understood?"

"Can I see it?" asked Millie.

"When it's finished," answered Mum. "Now, scoot, both of you."

The sewing machine whirred all morning. When Millie called Mum to lunch, she saw that the floor was covered with a sheet. Mum threw her sewing apron over the machine and the dress to keep them clean.

Early in the afternoon the machine's noise was replaced by a hymn. Millie knew Mum was practising the songs for the church choir's Easter concert while she did the hand sewing.

"Is it finished?" she asked at supper.

Mum rubbed her eyes. "Just another half-hour," she answered. "Come and see when you've done the dishes."

There it was, spread out on Mum's bed.

"Oh, it's beautiful!" breathed Millie as she stepped into the room.

"Don't touch!"

"I wasn't going to." Millie clasped her hands behind her back and gazed at the froth of white dotted organdy trimmed with lace and crisp blue bows. She imagined the girl who would be wearing it walking slowly down the aisle of the church in front of the bride. Everyone would be looking at them. She was brought back to reality by Mum's voice.

"The girl is just your age and your size," she said.

Responding to the longing in her daughter's face, Effie squeezed her shoulders. "Oh, Millie, I wish it was for you! You've been such a good child!" Releasing her, she added with a catch in her voice, "When we're rich, you shall have one just like it!"

"With blue bows?"

"Yes, and a blue sash. This one has an organdy sash, but they may decide on a blue ribbon. They hadn't made up their minds yesterday."

"The lace is so pretty," Millie said wistfully. Would they ever be rich enough for her to have lace trimming?

"Look," said Mum, "here's some left over. I'll sew it around the collar of your green dress for tomorrow. Then you'll have something new for Easter."

"But you're so tired, Mum."

"And that's God's truth!" she answered with a groan. "I'll just tack it on tonight and sew it permanently some day next week. How's that?"

When it was finished, Millie's dress looked pretty, but it was still an old one, and it was green and limp. Before she fell asleep, she imagined herself at a party wearing the crisp, white gown. Everyone, especially Lisette, would be so jealous!

The next day was warm enough to go to church without a coat. Everyone could see the new lace on Millie's dress. It couldn't compete, though, with Amy's whole new Easter outfit—pink dress, white hat, and buttoned shoes. Mrs. Brand and Amy were the best dressed people in church.

Just before they parted, Millie described for Amy the beautiful dress Mum had made.

Amy shivered happily. "It sounds wonderful! I wish I could see it."

Millie's mind raced. Here was a chance to get Amy to visit.

"Lisette's coming to see it this afternoon," she said eagerly. "Why don't you come, too?"

Amy looked down. She scraped a smooth patch in the gravel of the road with her boot.

"Mum will be at choir practice for the concert tonight, and Art will be playing soccer," Millie said.

Amy's foot was still.

"You've never seen such a pretty dress, even in the catalogue," coaxed Millie.

Amy looked up. "I'll come," she said.

When Lisette arrived just after two o'clock, Amy was already there. She stared coldly at the smaller girl while Millie nervously explained how she had described the dress to Amy and Amy had wanted to see it, too.

"Let's see it then," Lisette answered.

Millie hurried them into her mother's bedroom. She undid the package, spread the gown out on the bed, and stood back.

Both girls opened their eyes wide and sighed deeply.

"Is she going to be a bridesmaid? How old is she? Is she pretty?"

Millie happily answered all their questions. It felt so good for the three of them to be together.

After a few minutes, Amy said "I think the sash should be blue, to match the bows."

"It's a bit short," said Lisette. "How tall is this girl?"

"Mum says she's the same height as me," answered Millie.

"Then it's too short," Lisette declared.

"No, it isn't!" Millie snatched up the dress and held it against herself. "See? It's just right!"

"You can't tell that way. Try it on," Lisette dared her.

"No! I can't." Millie began to fold the dress.

"Too bad," said Amy.

The two girls turned towards the door. Were they going to leave?

"Wait!" Millie called. "I'll put it on for just a minute."

She wouldn't let either one of them touch it to help her except for tying the bow of the sash in the back.

"You look so pretty," sighed Amy.

"You're right," Lisette said. "It's just the right length. I know! Let's pretend we're at the party after the wedding! What do they do at weddings? Eat?"

"No!" yelled Millie, horrified at the thought of spilling.

"They dance," said Amy.

"Fun!" said Lisette. She ran out into the living room and opened the gramophone lid. "What will we play? Come on, Amy, you choose." She wound the crank vigorously. "Hurry up!"

Amy put on a waltz called "A Little Bit of Heaven."

"The bride and groom dance first," she said. "Then everyone else gets up."

Millie hesitated. She should change to her own clothes before playing. But the organdy dress seemed made for dancing. The skirt brushed against her legs temptingly as she swayed to the music. She found herself waltzing down the small room, turning in a swirl of white organdy, and waltzing back. The other two joined in. Amy held out her skirt with one hand. Lisette pretended to be holding a partner. Laughing, they dipped and swayed as they passed each other in the cramped space.

When the record began to slow down, all three were bunched up between the stove and the gramophone. In the scramble towards the crank, Millie's skirt brushed the sooty damper on the stove door.

Amy noticed it first.

Millie, following her horrified look, saw a black smudge just above the hem on the right side of the skirt. "Ooooooh!" she wailed.

"I have to go home now," said Lisette in a scared voice as she moved towards the front door.

Millie, followed by Amy, ran into the bedroom.

"Help me get out of it," she said.

In less than a minute Millie was back into her own clothes. She spread the organdy gown on the bed, and the two girls stood staring at the smudge. To them, it seemed very big and very black. Millie began to shiver, partly from fright and partly from remorse. What would the Marshall family say to Mum? And who would ever give her work after this? She groaned.

"Could we wash it?" asked Amy.

Millie just looked at her. It would take hours to heat water to wash it in, and hours longer to dry the dress. Besides, the organdy would lose its crisp newness.

"Why don't you just wrap it up again?" Amy suggested. "Maybe your Mum will think it happened on the train."

Millie's arm reached out eagerly, then dropped to her side. She couldn't do that. In her imagination, she saw Mum rubbing eyes strained by the close work. She saw her flexing her shoulders to ease the ache of bending

Wearing the organdy bridesmaid's dress, Millie dances with Amy.

for hours over the sewing machine. Oh, how could she have done such a wicked thing?

Just then, the door banged.

"We're home," shouted Ben.

The girls froze. They heard Mum, still singing. In a minute she would come into the bedroom to take off her hat.

Ben came first. He recognized the guilt on their faces. Looking for the cause, he saw the smudged dress lying on the bed.

"Ooh, you're going to get it!" he breathed.

"What for?" asked Mum gaily from the doorway.

The smile on her face faded. Red spots flared in her cheeks.

"Land sakes!" she shrieked. "What happened? Millie, what have you done?"

Millie sank to the floor and buried her head in her hands. She couldn't answer through the sobs that racked her whole body.

"We were playing wedding," Amy said timidly.

"Playing wedding? Who?"

"Lisette and Millie and me."

"But the dress!" wailed Effie.

"We wanted to see what it would look like on. Then we started dancing. And Millie touched the stove."

"Millie was wearing it?"

"Lisette dared her," said Amy.

For a long moment Millie's sobs were the only sound in the room. Then came a stern voice. "You'd better go, Amy."

"Yes, Mrs. Piggott. I'm sorry."

"You, too, Ben."

"But—"

"Go!"

Millie heard the door close and the chair creak as her mother sat down. She did not dare look up. Suddenly, inside her head, Dad said, "You've let me down, Millie. I thought better of my girl." She lowered her head to the floor, wishing for a hole she could sink into.

"Sit up, Millie," said Mum in a tired voice. "And stop that noise. Here, blow your nose."

Millie took the handkerchief Mum offered and tried hard to control her tears.

"I'm sorry, Mum."

"And so you should be! Now, don't start again! There's no use crying over spilt milk! We must decide how to mend the damage."

There was a tap on the door, and Art stuck his head in.

"Ben says Millie's in trouble. What did she do?" His eye caught the dress on the bed, and he walked in to examine the black mark. He swore. "Millie! After all Mum's hard work! You know she was counting on making a good impression. I thought you wanted us to get out of here?"

Tears poured down Millie's face.

"That's enough, Art," Effie said. "Millie's very, very sorry, and scolding won't do any good. Please go. I'm trying to think what to do to fix it."

"She should be—"

"Art! Please, if you want to help, get Ben something to eat."

With another frown at his sister, Art left.

Mum stood, picked up the sash of the dress, and measured it against the smudge. With a spark of hope in her heart, Millie pushed herself up.

"Can you fix it?" she asked with a tremor in her voice.

Mum began thinking out loud. "I'll cut out the dirty piece. If I unpick the sash, I'll have enough material to make a new panel. Then I'll trim the seam with lace. If I do the same on the other side, it will seem as if I planned it like that."

"Oh, Mum," breathed Millie.

Her mother looked at her sternly.

"You, young lady, will have to give back

the lace I put on your dress. Go and unpick it very carefully."

Millie ran off.

"And keep it clean!" Mum called after her.

It took all evening to repair the dress. Effie and Millie both missed the Easter music.

After school on Monday, Lisette and Amy were as anxious as Millie to hear what Mrs. Marshall had said.

"I'll go home and find out," Millie told them. "Meet me at the pump."

"The Marshalls didn't notice the change in the pattern," Effie said. "And they had already decided on a ribbon sash, so they didn't miss the organdy one."

Millie breathed a sigh of relief.

"But that doesn't excuse your behaviour. You had no right to touch that dress."

Millie hung her head.

"I'm sorry, Mum. I'll never do it again."

"You'll never get the chance!" Effie said. "Here's the pail. Go for water."

On the way to the pump, Millie met Lisette in the Gauthiers' own front yard.

"Whew! That's good!" Lisette said when she heard Millie's report. "But see what happens when you play with that Amy!"

"You were the one—" Millie began indignantly, but Lisette ran inside.

Amy was at the pump in the schoolyard. She, too, was relieved.

"I'm sorry you got into trouble with your Mum," she said.

She picked up her full pail and walked away.

"Can you come and play tomorrow?" Millie called after her.

"I don't think I'd better," answered Amy.

"Mum's not mad any more."

Amy shook her head and kept going.

For a moment Millie stared after her. Then she made a face. "Be like that!" she shouted. She turned to fill her own bucket. She hurried home so fast that the water splashed her legs and made her even madder. Who wants to be friends with a scab anyway? she thought.

Chapter Six

$\mathcal{T}$he next Sunday Dick Shepherd came to help Art dig the garden. Every spring Dad had spaded over the plot and planted the potatoes. Mum had sowed the rest of the vegetables, and the whole family had watered and weeded and killed bugs all summer.

Because of the unusually heavy snowfall during the winter, the ground had taken longer than usual to dry out enough to be dug. Mum was anxious to get the garden planted, and glad when Dick offered to help.

The two boys talked about the recent miners' meeting. As an aid to the war effort, all the collieries on the Island, from Cumberland in the north to South Wellington in the south, had decided to ask their employees to go all-out one day to produce a record number of tons of coal. Since the men who worked on the face were paid for the coal they dug, they would earn extra money. The Company would match every dollar of the extra money that the miners donated to the Red Cross. The mine that exceeded its usual output by the most would be awarded a plaque.

Dick's father had been at the meeting.

"Bart Menzies is against it," Dick reported. "He says it's just a plot by the Companies to get more work out of the men. He told them if they increased production one day they'd be expected to do it every day. My Dad says he gave a right bitter speech, bringing up the strike all over again."

"He's got cause to be bitter," said Art. "He was in jail for eighteen months."

"Yeah, and he didn't do anything worse than many who got off."

"Not as bad," Art agreed. "But he was strong for the Union. The Company was out to get him."

"Yeah. Bart will never work in the pits again. He's blacklisted everywhere."

"I wonder why he stays here?"

"Likes to stick around and bug the Company, I guess," Dick answered. "Like speaking against them at the meeting."

Art wiped his sweaty face on his sleeve.

He wished he were as strong as Dick, who had dug almost twice as much without seeming to feel tired. He pushed the spade in again. At least it was easier than digging coal. No dust, either.

"I hear the men went along with it," he said.

Dick laughed. "Well, the Company's got us over a barrel, eh? They say, do this for the war effort. If you say no, you're a traitor."

One morning a large notice was posted on the lamphouse wall. May 10th was the day chosen for the contest. The output of the night shift, which began at eleven o'clock on the 9th, would be counted first. Dick was reading the poster as Art came up.

"We're going to make the coal fly that day!" he boasted. "Those other mines haven't got a chance!"

Art grinned at him, but inside he cringed. Dad always used to say that most mine accidents happened when the men got careless. Would they forget safety when they were rushing to win the contest?

At seven o'clock on May 10th, the pit boss himself stressed safety in his pep talk to the men.

"No sense winning putting out more coal,

if it puts out lives," he said. "Safety first, as always. You can see those guys last night really moved the coal. Three hundred and fifty tons!" He punched his fist into the air. "We can do even better! Let's give the next shift something to shoot for!"

"Aye! Aye!" the men responded. Many imitated his salute.

Art was so caught up in the excitement that he almost forgot his fears. Besides, he was so busy he had no time to brood. Cars clattered past the winch all day. Some old or broken ones had been hauled back to work on this special day. Many of these slipped off the track. If a full car derailed, it was the rope-rider's job to put it back. But if an empty went off as it came up from below, Art had to slue it back on. He would take a metal lever, brace it under the axle, and heave with all his strength. He lost count of how many times he'd done it by the end of the shift. His aching shoulders told him it was too many.

The weigh man kept a running total of the number of tons of coal. When the men streamed wearily out of the adit, they were greeted by a big sign showing they had far exceeded their usual ouput, with more cars still to be counted. Grinning triumphantly, they called challenges to the men of the next shift.

After his bath, Mum rubbed liniment into Art's stiff shoulders.

"I hope all the effort was worth it," she said grimly.

The next day the miners found out that it had been. A banner hung on the office wall.

EXTENSION WINS!
1,044 Tons!
25% INCREASE!

Dick cheered wildly.

"Don't count your chickens yet," Art warned.

He was reading the fine print at the bottom of the notice which listed each mine's output from the day before.

"Why not?" Dick demanded.

"Read it out, kid," called another miner.

Art obeyed. "The final totals will be calculated after the completion of work on May 11th. Any discrepancy between that day's tonnage and the average tonnage will be deducted from the contest total."

Several men swore. "What's that mean?" asked one.

"It means no slacking off," growled the pit boss. "So quit patting yourselves on the back, and get to work!"

Men cursed and grumbled.

One voice rose above the others. "By gum, let's do it! The Company said they'd match our donation to the Red Cross. Make them pay every cent!"

Although some men agreed with him, it was not a happy crew that moved towards the mine. Just before Art reached the entrance, he heard a great shout. With other men, he paused and looked toward the slag pile. Standing on top of it was Bart Menzies. He held a long board on which he had printed a word in charcoal: SUCKERS.

As the day wore on Art knew that the miners were digging the usual amount of coal. The old cars had not all been sorted out yet. Twice, he had to lift derailed cars. Both times, his muscles screamed with pain. He prayed that he wouldn't have to slue another for he was afraid he wouldn't be able to do it. He would be ashamed to have to ask Dick for help with an empty.

— About two hours before the end of the shift, Dick signalled again for the hoist. As he passed, he waved from his perch on the rope between the first and the second cars in a train of six. The final car was poised on the top of the slope when Art heard the dreaded clank of a wheel jumping the track. The winch stopped moving. Out of the darkness came a prolonged scream.

Art quickly threw the lever to brake the car, and turned off the winch switch. Then he raced down towards the sound of Dick's voice. His stomach was heaving with nausea as the light from his headlamp bounced crazily off the walls of the tunnel.

"Me arm! Me arm!" moaned Dick.

It was the second car which had derailed. Dick's feet were on the ground, but his upper right arm was caught between the two cars. He was helpless.

"Get it off me, Art!"

I can't, thought Art. I can't lift a full car. At the same time he reached for the prying lever that a rope-rider always carried. Praying for strength, he managed to move the heavy load a bare inch and hold it there.

Meanwhile, Dick was yelling for help.

"Heave!" he pleaded. "You can do it, Art. I don't want to lose my arm!"

Art knew he couldn't do it. In a few seconds he would have to let go and the weight would drop onto Dick again.

The sound of feet pounding up from the main tunnel and shouts from the blackness beyond the winch gave him the courage to hang on. In a moment, stronger hands than his grasped the pry bar. He stepped back on trembling legs and leaned against a post. Three men freed his friend. They repositioned the car and examined Dick's injury, then ordered Dick to the doctor and Art back to the winch. Within fifteen minutes the coal was moving again.

Art's hands trembled for much longer than that. He couldn't stop thinking about Dick. Would his arm have to be amputated? If he lost it, there went his dream of being a miner like his Dad. When the quitting whistle finally blew, Art almost ran out of the mine. He did not even bother to glance at the board beside the weigh scale. Who cared if the shift had made its quota that day? All he wanted was to get home, wash off the coal, and not think about the mine for a few hours.

After tea, he tried burying himself in a book, but the memory of Dick's sweat-beaded face and pleading voice kept intruding.

About seven o'clock, Dick's voice shouted from the front gate. Art raced to open the door.

Dick held up his plaster cast and grinned. "Doc says you saved my arm. It's broken, of course, but any more pressure and she'd have been too crushed to save. Don't look so scared! I'm telling you you're a hero!"

"Hero!" gasped Art. "Me? A little weakling that can't even slue a car!"

"You were strong enough for me," his friend answered. "And did you hear we made our quota? We're going to win that contest, but I don't know how you guys are going to get along without me for a month."

Art laughed with relief. It seemed nothing could quench his pal's enthusiasm for mining.

Dick strutted when the outcome of the contest was finally determined. Extension was the clear winner. The plaque would be presented at the big Miner's Picnic in Nanaimo on May 24th, and Dick planned to be there.

Chapter Seven

*A*ll the collieries on the Island ran excursion trains to Nanaimo for the Empire Day celebrations on May 24th. Aunt Helen had written to urge the Piggotts to come and picnic with her and Uncle Stan.

"I'm sure you must all be ready for a bit of fun," she wrote. "There will be plenty for the children to do, and we can have a good visit."

"She's right," said Mum. "We all deserve a holiday. We'll go."

Ben was ready an hour before the train was to leave. About a year ago he had seen a parade in Ladysmith in which clowns had thrown candy to children. Millie told him that this parade would be even bigger and better. He expected to find the street paved with suckers and gumballs.

He was disappointed in that, but forgot it in his delight at the parade, which he watched from his perch on Art's shoulders. There were soldiers, bands, floats, horses, cars, and people dressed as characters from the comics and the movies.

Suddenly, he pounded his fists on Art's head.

"Look! Look! Mutt and Jeff are throwing candy! I want down! Put me down!"

"Gladly!" said Art.

"Go with him, Millie," Mum called as Ben darted into the scrimmage on the street.

Ben felt his sister tugging on his shirt, but he didn't move back until his hands were crammed full of paper-covered toffees.

"Your aunt and uncle have gone ahead to the park to find a shady place to picnic," Mum said. "Stay with us, Ben. We'd never find you in this crowd. Millie, you hold onto him."

There were about four thousand people in the park, all busy arranging themselves around a cleared space in the middle. On one side a platform had been built. Later in the day speeches would be made from it, and races and games for children and a first aid competition held in front of it. In the field behind the platform, various miners' teams would hold a baseball tournament.

Lunch first. But how to find Aunt Helen and Uncle Stan? Everywhere Ben looked groups of people were spreading blankets and tablecloths on the ground and setting out food.

A high, shrill voice cut across all the other greetings and calls. "Yoohoo! Effie! Millie!"

"That's Aunt Helen," Millie said.

Ben spotted her waving a white hankie, and took off at a run.

Uncle Stan caught him under the arms, lifted him over his head, and twirled him round and round. Ben squealed as the sports field, the town, and the islands far below spun in circles.

"Hello, young Ben," boomed his uncle as he set him down.

Still dizzy, Ben felt his aunt's bony arms clasp him tightly. She planted a dry kiss on his cheek. Ben squirmed out of her reach and stared at the feast spread out on the chequered tablecloth. There were two plates of sandwiches, a mountain of potato salad, a dish of pickles, a flat sponge cake, a huge, round cake

---

Ben eats more than his fill at the Empire Day picnic.

with chocolate icing, and two jars of lemonade. Ben had helped pack almost as much in the baskets Mum and Art were carrying.

The two women sat on camp stools, and the rest of them sprawled on the ground. After about half an hour of steady eating, Ben eyed the chocolate cake wondering whether he had room for one more piece.

Mum shook her head at him. "No more, Ben. You'll be too full to run in the races."

Just then, a trumpet blew. They turned to see the platform full of men.

"They're going to give out the plaque we won," said Art.

Ben dragged Millie over to stand with Jackie and Lisette. None of them listened to the speeches, but they cheered with everybody else when Mr. Warbell, the manager, accepted the plaque for the Extension mine.

Then the Nanaimo Brass Band climbed onto the stage.

Recognizing the blue uniforms with the red braid trim, Ben said, "Look, Millie. We saw them before. Is there going to be another parade?"

"No, something else," she answered.

With their instruments glistening in the sun, the band began to play "Colonel Bogie."

Over a hundred school children marched out from behind the bandstand and lined the square. The girls wore white dresses, and the boys white shirts. Each child held a piece of cardboard chest high. Some of the squares were red, some white, and some blue. Two of the red squares stopped in front of Ben.

"I can't see anything," he complained.

"Sssh!" said Millie.

At a signal from the bandmaster, the children began an intricate set of marching maneuvers. They marched into a coil, then undid it. They formed squares by colour. They crisscrossed the field, weaving their lines in and out. When the music ended with a clash of cymbals, they were bunched together in a rectangular shape.

"Tan-ta-ra," blared the trumpet.

The children all raised their cardboard squares over their heads. They had formed a Union Jack flag with its blue background and red and white crosses.

Behind Ben, Millie gasped in surprise and delight. The crowd cheered and clapped. The band played music that sounded like the wind blowing, and the children swayed to and fro. It looked as if the flag were waving in the breeze.

"I wish we could do that," Millie said. "Oh, Lisette, let's ask Miss Gall if we can!"

"We don't have enough kids," Lisette said.

"Not for a flag, maybe, but we could do a drill!"

"We don't have a band."

"Jack Hodges plays the drum. And Miss Gall can play the piano. Wouldn't you like to do that?"

She had to shout over the cheering of the crowd as the children marched away.

"Yes, but—"

"Look!" interrupted Jackie. "They're getting ready for the races!"

Ben lined up with Jackie for the boys under six straight race. He saw his mother on the sidelines, gave her a quick, nervous grin, then crouched in position.

"On your marks! Get set! Go!"

Millie had coached him. "When you're running," she'd said, "don't look back. Keep your eyes on the string at the end, and run like blazes!"

Ben did just that, and came in second.

A man tapped him on the shoulder and led him over to a table where another man sat with a plateful of coins.

"A nickle for the winner, three cents for

second, and two cents for third," he said. "Well done all!"

Ben stared at the coins in his hand. He didn't know you could earn money by racing!

He took out his handkerchief, wrapped the three coins with care, and shoved the bundle deep into the corner of his pants' pocket. He hoped to add lots more to it.

He and Jackie finished out of the money in the three-legged race, but they won the wheelbarrow run. Jackie wanted to use the nickel to buy an ice cream cone to share, but Ben had a plan for his money. He gave Jackie three cents, and kept two pennies himself. He won another three cents for coming second in the potato sack hop.

That was the last race for boys his age. He stayed on the sidelines for a few minutes to watch Millie, but got bored and wandered away. Something was going on behind the platform. A long table and benches had been set up. The table was covered with pies, and the benches were filled with men and boys.

"Pie eating contest! Be a champion! Win a prize!" called a man with a megaphone.

Dad had always called Ben the champion tart-eater. It should be easy to win this. He nipped into the last vacant place. There was a full size apple pie in front of him, and two more lined up behind it.

"On your marks! Go!"

Half way through the pie, Ben slowed down. He thought of the potato salad, the four sandwiches, the six pickles, and the three pieces of cake he'd eaten for lunch. The very last bite wouldn't go down. Some men had finished their three pies and had three more lined up. Ben knew he was beaten. He might as well leave, but he couldn't move just yet.

The winner ate seven and a half pies. He won twenty-five cents. The man giving out the prizes stopped in front of Ben.

"And two cents to the youngest contestant," he said. As he handed over the coins, he said, "You look pale. Are you feeling all right, kid?"

Ben nodded. He stood up slowly and walked carefully over to the baseball field and sat down on the sidelines. For a few minutes, he couldn't think of anything except his stomach. Then a great shout made him look up in time to see two runners score on a home run by the Extension team. They had won the game! He saw Art on the edge of the crowd of men shaking hands and slapping backs.

From behind him, Millie said, "So here you are! Come on. Mum wants you."

"What for?"

Millie shrugged. "She wants to know where you are, I guess."

The three adults were sitting at a small table under the awning of the tea marquee.

"Hold out your hand, Mum," said Ben.

He unfolded his handkerchief carefully and counted ten pennies into her hand.

"Thank you, son," Mum said. "Where on earth did you get all these pennies?"

"I won them all," he said with pride. "They're to get Art out of the mine."

Uncle Stan's boom of laughter made Ben shrivel.

"That little bit's not going to be much help," his aunt said with a shrill titter. "You'd better spend it on ice cream."

Ben shrank into the fold of his mother's arm.

His uncle cleared his throat. "You don't need to spend your money on ice cream," he said. "I've got a special fund for that right here in my vest pocket. Been saving all week. We'll all have cones with our tea before you catch your train."

Mum kissed the top of Ben's head. "Every little bit counts," she said. "I'm glad you want to help."

"Here are my pennies, too!" said Millie, putting the money into Effie's hands. "We are going to get Art out of the mine!" she said to Aunt Helen.

Aunt Helen sighed. "Well, I hope so. It's what your Dad wanted. And your Granddad, too. He was saving his money, as well, Ben, in an old tobacco tin."

"I knew Granddad had a box!" Millie cried.

Ben looked up from the shelter of his mother's arm. His sister's eyes were shining.

"Oh, yes," said Aunt Helen. "For as long as I can remember, he kept a bit extra in his tin box."

"It was square and yellow, and it had a picture on it," declared Millie, who could suddenly see it in her mind's eye. Her mother was holding it and reaching towards...towards what? Oh! She had almost seen where her mother had hidden it!

"Fancy you remembering," Aunt Helen said. "My Dad had to empty the box when he and I came out from England to join your Dad. But then Dad started a new one. And you're right, it was yellow, but it was more oblong than square. The picture was of three ladies' heads. Do you remember that?"

Millie shook her head. Aunt Helen laughed.

"The tobacco was called Three Twins Fine Cut. I always thought that was queer. When I married your Uncle Stan, Dad gave most of his savings to me. Not that it was all that much, but, still, it's the thought that counts."

"Aye," said Uncle Stan. "He was glad she was marrying a man who had quit the mine and gone into the hauling business. He didn't want Art underground, that's for certain."

"From the time Art was a baby, Dad always said his savings were to give the boy an education so he wouldn't have to go into the mine," said Aunt Helen with a sigh. "I suppose it was all used up in the strike, Effie?"

Mum nodded, but Millie said, "Maybe not! Maybe the box is still hidden somewhere!"

"Not likely!" said Uncle Stan.

The adults all laughed. Ben didn't. Millie was good at finding things. Maybe she would find Granddad's box.

Chapter Eight

$\mathcal{A}$t school the next day, Millie and Lisette found that Miss Gall had been as excited by the flag drill as they were. She said she had watched it with other teachers from South Wellington and Ladysmith, and they had decided to combine forces to present something similar at the Miners' Picnic in Ladysmith on Dominion Day.

"We don't have enough children to make a flag," she said, "but we can do a patriotic drill using red, white, and blue sashes." She flapped open a long, wide strip of white cotton. "They'll go over your left shoulder, like this, and tie around your waist on the right side. See?"

"Will ours all be white?" asked Lisette.

"No," answered the teacher. "Our colour is blue. We need twelve children, but I have enough material to make only six sashes. If any of you have something suitable at home, please bring it. I'll buy some blue dye so that they'll all be the same shade. Now, to choose the marchers. Is anyone not going to the Miners' Picnic?"

As usual, all the families were going. Miss Gall decided to leave out the youngest children. John Pawley, the oldest, said it was kid's stuff. So grades four, five, and six were chosen. The first practice was held at recess the next day.

After three practices, the teacher chose Millie and Amy to be the leaders of the two groups. Frank snorted, and Lisette made a face. Miss Gall frowned at them. "They are the best at remembering the movements," she said firmly.

Frank was in Amy's group. At first, whenever the teacher wasn't looking, he made mistakes. Millie and some of the others yelled at him and he seemed to settle down, but Millie didn't like the sly grin he wore every time they drilled. If he was going to be mean, she was going to stick up for Amy.

After one Friday practice, she invited Amy to play with her on Saturay afternoon when chores were finished. She also asked Lisette, who refused with a sneer.

Saturday was another warm, sunny day. Fortunately, Lisette and Frank were both elsewhere when Amy walked quickly past their house after lunch.

"I've just got one more chore to do," Millie said as she greeted Amy at the scullery door. She picked up two parcels wrapped in newspaper. "I have to take this mending to the hotel. Will you come with me?"

The hotel, the only two-storey building in Extension, was across the railroad tracks. The girls threaded their way past the coal cars. They reached the platform just as Frank Gauthier picked up the handles of a loaded wheelbarrow. It was full of food supplies that the hotel cook had ordered from the stores in Ladysmith.

"He's going to be mad," Frank said to the railway clerk.

"So what?" asked the man. "It's not my fault. We can't ship him strawberries if there aren't any in town."

"I'm the one he'll yell at," said Frank, moving away.

Frank paid no attention to the two girls

Millie and Amy walk through the streets of Extension to the hotel.

who followed him up the hill. At the hotel he pushed his wheelbarrow around to the kitchen door at the back.

Avoiding the noisy bar, Millie and Amy went up the broad front steps, across the verandah, and into the dark, empty hall. Millie exchanged the neatly wrapped bundles for the two untidy ones lying on the wooden counter. A roar came from the kitchen. The girls grinned at one another. A moment later, they saw Frank trundling his wheelbarrow down the slope at a run. Giggling, they turned to follow him. A door to the left of the counter swung open violently, and a tall Chinese man strode in. He was wearing a very long, white apron and a white, wedge cap which had slipped over his left ear. He glared around the empty hall, and then at the girls.

"Where's the boss?" he demanded.

Amy clutched Millie's arm.

Millie was scared, too, but she managed to blurt out, "We haven't seen him!"

"How can I make pies?" demanded the cook. "No lemons! No strawberries!"

Strawberries! Millie had a bright idea. Ever since the day with Aunt Helen, she had been trying to think of an excuse to go to the old house. She knew Mum and Art would laugh at her if she said she wanted to search for Granddad's box, and she hadn't wanted to go alone. But Amy was with her now.

She met the man's eyes. "I know where there are some strawberries," she said. "My friend and I can get you some."

"Millie!" Amy groaned.

Millie looked at her coaxingly. "You know, Amy. Up where we used to live. Both our gardens had big strawberry patches. Nobody goes there anymore. There must be plenty."

"You pick, I pay," the cook said. "Come."

He walked back through the swinging door. Millie put down the parcels of mending, grabbed Amy's arm, and dragged her after him. The kitchen was crammed with well-used furniture and equipment, but it was shining clean. The tall man lifted down two enamel colanders from the top row of an assortment of pans hanging on one wall.

Holding them out toward the girls, he said, "Two bits."

Amy didn't move, so Millie took both pans.

Safely outside, she said, "Wow! Twenty-five cents!"

"Why did you say we'd do it?" scolded Amy. "The gardens must be full of weeds by now. There won't be any berries."

"We can at least look, can't we?"

Millie started up the hill. Amy trailed behind.

"We'll never fill those things, and he'll be mad," she said.

"I'll take them back," Millie assured her.

"Cross your heart?"

"Yes. I'll have to get the mending anyway. Come on!"

They ran past the big rock where Ben and some other kids were playing King of the Castle, and past the last house on John Street, until they came to the road where they had both been born. They stopped and stared. Their street, Ogden, ran at right angles to John. They could see the whole length of the sunlit road, from the bush separating it from Chinatown at one end, to the forest at the other.

Amy hadn't been over to this side of town since the night her family had been attacked by the mob. The first summer after their move, Millie had come once with Mum to pick berries, but now they had a larger patch in their own yard. The street looked different somehow. Millie remembered six houses, almost exactly alike. They were rectangular in shape, like white wooden boxes with shingled roofs for lids. Each had a porch in front and a wash-room added to one back corner, but their front doors had been painted different colours. The Piggots' was red.

Before Millie's parents were married, the miners had moved from Wellington to the new mine at Extension, and these houses had been cut in half, loaded on flat cars, and brought by rail to the new town. One man had added a stone chimney and a fireplace to the front room when he put his house together again. This was the house Wilf Piggott rented. The chimney and the red door made it easy for Millie to know her own home. But now it looked all wrong.

"It's scary," said Amy. "The houses look like jails. See the boards nailed over the doors and the windows? And the paint's all coming off." She shivered. "Let's go home."

Millie grabbed her arm as she turned away. "No!" The houses did look spooky, but now that she was this close to being able to look for Granddad's box, she wasn't going to give up. "Don't you want to earn the twenty-five cents?"

"Look at the yards," Amy protested. "The grass is so high, and there are vines all over.

The backyards must be bush."

"Let's go and see," said Millie.

She crossed the dirt road that was dotted with yellow dandelions and buttercups. The drainage ditch, now bone-dry, was overgrown with sweet smelling clover and purple rocket. Since no rain had fallen for a month, all the colours were dulled by dust. In front of the Brands' old house the board spanning the ditch looked rotten on the edges. The centre held Millie. From the other side of the ditch, she looked back at her friend.

"You're a sissy, Amy Brand!"

Amy scowled and tossed her head. "Am not!"

"Prove it!"

In a minute, the two girls were in the backyard of the former Brand house. The forest undergrowth had crept down the mountain into the garden. But, beneath the weeds and the thistles, they found large, luscious, ripe berries.

"I told you so!" said Millie. She spat on a berry, rubbed off the dust with her finger, and popped it into her mouth. "Mmmm! Yummy!"

They ate two each, then settled to the task of filling the colanders. When they could find no more berries in that patch, they ducked through a gap in the rotting fence.

Once more, Millie stood in her own garden. As she stared at the house, she felt very sure that somewhere inside was Granddad's box. In her imagination, she walked through the four rooms. She pictured herself as a little girl sitting on the kitchen couch watching her mother and her grandfather open the box, put something in, and close it. She even heard the tiny click of the metal lid. But she could not remember where they had put it! Surely if she could get inside, the hiding place would come to her.

"There are some berries over here," Amy called. "Get picking! I want to get out of here."

Millie obeyed, but all the time she worked she kept glancing at the house, trying to figure out how to get Amy to go in with her. It was spooky up here at the edge of town under the shadow of the mountain. By the time their berries reached the highest row of holes in the second colander, the whole garden was in shadow. Amy wouldn't stay much longer. Millie glanced towards the house to see whether it was still in sunlight. Just then, a man came around from the side path. Millie gasped.

"What?" asked Amy, looking up. "Oh!"

she squeaked. She dropped her handful of berries, and ducked into the weeds.

"Who are you? What are you doing?" the man demanded. He was thin and unshaven. Grey hair hung in uneven strands below his ears. There were patches on the knees of his pants, and a hole in the elbow of his plaid shirt.

"Hello, Mr. Menzies," said Millie bravely. "I'm Millie Piggott."

"Wilf Piggott's kid?" The man's voice was friendlier.

Millie nodded. "This used to be our garden."

"I knew yer Dad. Yer Grandfather was my mate. Hugh Piggott was a fine man." His voice hardened again. "You shouldn't be here."

"We're picking strawberries," Millie protested.

"Don't you know this street is unsafe? There's going to be a cave-in here some day. You'd think the Company would warn little kids, but oh, no! They're not going to admit they mined too close to the surface. Not them!

Millie wonders where in her grandfather's old house his tin box of money might be.

101

But I'm telling you. Go off home now!"

Millie tucked one full colander into the crook of her arm. Amy grabbed the other, then reached out for Millie's hand. Sidling around Bart Menzies, the two girls walked quickly past the house.

The old man followed them. "And don't you come back, you hear?" he called fiercely across the road.

When they had gone almost a block down John Street, Amy let out a long breath.

"I'm glad you didn't tell him my name. He'd have killed me," she said.

"Don't be silly!" Millie answered. "He's fierce against the Company and the men who kept working during the strike," she almost called them scabs, "but he wouldn't hurt us."

Amy didn't argue, but she dropped Millie's hand.

"Anyway, we got the strawberries," Millie went on cheerfully. "Did you see all the flowers on the raspberry canes? I'll bet the cook will buy those, too. We'll go back in July to pick them."

"Not me!" declared Amy. "Mr. Menzies said it wasn't safe up there."

"Oh, he just said that to scare us off," said Millie. "He's not allowed on Company property, you know. He doesn't want anyone to find out he's living in our house."

Amy stopped and stared at her friend. "Is he? How do you know?"

"Didn't you notice the boards were off the back door and one of the windows? There was a full pail of water on the stoop, and a bit of the garden was planted with potatoes. I could smell bacon, too."

"Wow!" said Amy. "You're a real detective! I didn't see any of that."

"I did," said Millie, "and I'm not scared of him. I'm going back when the raspberries are ripe."

She spoke more bravely than she felt. Still, why shouldn't her grandfather's friend let her look for her grandfather's box?

At the hotel, the cook chuckled over the berries and gave Millie two dimes and a nickel.

When Millie rejoined her friend outside, Amy said, "You keep the nickel. It was your idea."

Millie was glad to add money to the family savings. She was happier still to know that the old house was not completely boarded up. She just had to find the right time to go back and the courage to get in.

Chapter Nine

*E*arly on the morning of July 1, the two public wells in Extension went dry. All through the day before, mothers had been washing clothes and bathing children for the picnic. Those who were last in line at the pump on the big day had to make do with a lick and a promise.

Ben didn't even get that. He started out clean, and was told to sit still and stay that way while the rest of the family packed the lunch and the swimming things. But the one thing Ben couldn't do when he was excited was sit still. He went in search of his friend Jackie.

When the train blew the warning whistle, the three Piggots stepped out of the house. Ben was not in the yard. They hurried on to the Gauthiers' expecting to find him there. That family was looking back towards the Piggotts, waiting for Jackie to appear.

"Where can they be?" Mrs. Gauthier asked crossly.

"Wait for us!" came a yell from the slag pile. Two grubby little boys raced towards their clean, dressed-up families. Their teeth, bared in wide grins, showed very white against their sooty faces. They held out black hands to be clasped. Everyone drew back with a cry.

Ben's grin changed to a pout. "You took so long," he whined. "We went to play."

The Gauthiers blamed Ben; the Piggotts blamed Jackie.

Pete Gauthier grabbed a hand of each child.

"Get a move on, all of you, or we'll miss the train," he said. "We'll throw these two into the sea when we get there."

Millie wasn't there to see that. The children who were in the drill had been told to go straight from the Ladysmith station to the school ground. There was to be a practice of the drill with all the schools so that they'd know what to do at the actual performance in the afternoon.

As Millie, Lisette, and Amy plodded up the steep street, Frank darted past them.

Turning his head, he jeered at Amy. "Nyah, nyah! You couldn't lead a horse to water."

"Don't you dare, Frank!" Lisette yelled at his bounding back.

"What's he up to?" Millie demanded.

Lisette just shrugged.

South Wellington School had not yet arrived at the field, so they were told to wait. Millie looked down over the town. Although it was smaller than Nanaimo, compared to Extension, Ladysmith was a city. Residential streets like steps filled the steep slope from the shoreline to the forest on the mountain above. On one street, both sides were filled with stores, including the millinery where Mum worked. Down at the waterfront, there was a train station made of brick and three hotels, one of which was three storeys tall. But the largest building to be seen was the coal washing plant at the head of the harbour. Near it were three huge wharves. Several freighters were anchored in the harbour waiting until after the holiday to dock at the wharves and load coal to deliver to far-off ports.

No doubt there was plenty of coal dust down on the waterfront, but up here the air was clear. This was the street of Millie's dreams. If they could live here, Art would be safe.

She felt a tap on her shoulder and turned. Amy introduced her to her cousin, Prudence Brand, a tall, thin girl who didn't seem to know what to do with her long arms and legs. When it came to marching, though, she was the cleverest of them all. No wonder she had been chosen to lead the whole troop. To the embarrassment of Extension School, it was Amy's line which spoiled the first practice drill. Everyone ended up in a big muddle in the middle of the field. The man in charge sent all the groups back to their starting positions.

While the teachers conferred, Amy defended herself to the other pupils. "It was Frank's fault," she said. "He turned the wrong way. He's doing it on purpose."

"Who, me?" asked Frank innocently. "I was just following your lead."

Lisette scolded him in her best big-sister voice, but he just grinned.

Millie was furious. Of course he was doing it on purpose to hurt Amy. What he really wanted was to force Amy to give the lead place to Lisette. No! No! No! How could she stop him? There was no use threatening him with the teacher. School was over for the summer, and Miss Gall was not coming back in September.

Just then, Prue Brand strolled over.

"How come you kids messed up?" she asked.

"Frank's making mistakes on purpose," Amy answered in a tight voice.

Her face had gone white and still, as it always did when she was trying not to cry.

"He's going to ruin the drill!" Millie said angrily.

Prue looked from her cousin to the smirking boy.

"He'd better not," she said.

"Who's going to stop me?" Frank demanded.

Prue stuck two fingers in her mouth, and blew a sharp, shrill whistle. In a moment, she was joined by a boy who must have been her twin brother. He was taller and much heavier than Prue.

"This here's my brother Caleb. Listen, Cale, this kid's got it in for our Amy. He's going to mess up the drill."

"Which kid?" asked her brother in a deep voice.

Prue nodded at Frank.

Caleb droped a huge hand onto the blue

sash over the younger boy's shoulder. "Naw, he wouldn't do that! Would you, kid?"

His voice was teasing, but his stare was hard. Frank tried to pull away. The strong fingers dug deeper.

Lisette moved to her brother's side. "Leave him alone, you big bully," she said. "He'll do it right."

A whistle blew and the scattered children ran to their places. This time the rehearsal went perfectly. The marchers handed in their sashes and were dismissed to join their families in the park by the sea.

"Want to stop home for a drink of lemonade?" Prue asked Amy, Millie, and Lisette.

"No, thanks," said Lisette coldly. She ran to join some others who were racing down the hill.

Millie went with the cousins.

The Brand house turned out to be Millie's dream house. As soon as she stepped inside, she began to imagine her family living there. The downstairs was divided into four rooms, just like the house in Extension, except that the hallway was wide enough for a real staircase.

"Do they have an upstairs, Amy?" she whispered.

"Yes, but we can't go up. That's where the boarders sleep."

So the place was big enough to take in boarders who could help pay the rent! It was perfect!

"I like your house, Prue," she said, as she took the glass the girl handed her.

"Me, too," answered Prue. "I hope the new one's as big."

Surprised, Amy asked, "Are you moving?"

"Dad'll have his explosives certificate by the end of the summer. He's going to be a shot boss in Cumberland."

Amy looked sad. "Oh, then I won't be able to visit you after this."

Prue wagged her finger. "Don't borrow trouble," she said in imitation of her mother's voice. She laughed. "Cheer up! You're going to be here for two weeks. We'll have lots of fun."

Walking down to the park, the two cousins discussed their plans for Amy's visit. Millie was busy with her own thoughts. Wouldn't it

---

The Brand boarding house in Ladysmith is Millie's dream house.

---

be wonderful if they could rent the house when the Brands moved? The house was perfect, and the timing just right. Mum always said they'd move to Ladysmith at the end of August.

As soon as the girls reached the park they changed into their bathing suits and raced into the water. Millie found Ben blue with cold. No trace of coal soot remained. Through chattering teeth, he said he'd been swimming since they arrived, but he wasn't ready to come out yet. He was having too much fun. She managed to drag him to the hot stones of the beach before the noon whistle blew. This was partly to save him from turning to ice, and partly because she wanted to talk to Mum.

She told her all about the Brand house. Mum said she'd talk to Mrs. Brand before the train left that evening.

"Why not now?" asked Millie.

"Because it's time to eat."

"Yeah! I'm starved," interrupted Ben.

"Where's Art?" Effie asked.

"I haven't seen him," Millie answered.

"Oh, well, he'll turn up. We can't let poor Ben die of hunger. Dig in, son."

Art arrived just in time to take the last jam tart from Ben's hand.

"No fair!" said the little boy. "Mum, if he's late, he should go without, shouldn't he?"

"You've probably had four or five already," Art said.

"I've only had three!" answered Ben.

"Anyway, I've been busy," said Art.

"What at?" asked Millie. She handed him a packet of sandwiches.

"First, I went to see Mr. Archibald at the Feed Store. He's a friend of Uncle Stan's. Say, these are all cheese sandwiches. Aren't there any beef?"

Mum passed him the tin. "Why did you want to see him?" she asked.

"To ask him for a job, in case we come to Ladysmith in September. He said he'd give me one."

"Doing what?" asked Millie. She had to wait while he chewed and swallowed.

"Odd jobs. Sweeping up and running errands. Things like that."

"What about school?" asked Mum in a worried voice.

"Well, after I talked to Mr. Archibald, I met Mr. Stronk. You know him, he was the teacher at Extension three years ago."

"I remember. He always said you were his best pupil," Mum answered with pride.

"Maybe," mumbled Art. "Anyway, he says he'll help me keep up so I can enter high school next year. That is, if we move here."

"We will! We will!"

Millie jumped up from the bench and danced around the table. "Oh, Mum! It's all going to work out! We'll live in the Brands' house, and you and Art will have work, and the boarders will pay us, and we'll save lots and lots of money, and Art can go back to school and be a doctor or a teacher or something, not a miner! Hurray! Hurray!"

"Don't count your chickens before they're hatched," warned Mum.

"Don't run around like a chicken with its head cut off," said Art.

Laughing loudly, Ben followed Millie. He made wings of his arms and flapped them as he ran.

"Squawk! Squawk! Squawk! " he yelled.

"Simmer down, you two," ordered their older brother. "Look, Millie, Lisette's calling you."

She stopped so abruptly that Ben crashed into her.

"Oh! Time for the drill. Come and watch, Mum."

With Caleb Brand also watching from the

sidelines, the drill went off with a hitch and the show was a great success. Amy caught Millie's eye and smiled with relief, and everybody told the children how proud they were of them.

On the train going home, Ben fell asleep on Mum's lap, his shirt full of ribbons he had won in that day's races and games. Millie cuddled up to Effie's free shoulder. Just as she'd promised, Effie had spoken to the Brands and arranged to see the owner of their house the next time she was in Ladysmith.

"This has been a perfect day," Millie murmured. "Finding the house. Art's job. It's all perfect."

"Everything does seem to be going our way," Mum agreed cautiously, "but let's not tempt fate. Our savings are so small. We might not be able to afford to move. Let's just say, if nothing goes wrong, we may have Art out of the mine by the end of August."

"Oh, Mum," Millie groaned. "Don't be like that!" She nestled closer and rubbed her cheek on her mother's sleeve. "We will make it!"

Mum sighed. "Keep your dreams, child," she said. "If we couldn't dream, life would be pretty bleak."

Chapter Ten

The summer of 1916 was a hard one in Extension. To begin with, the war news was bad. Several families grieved for soldiers who had been reported killed or missing in action. And there was no break in the dry, hot weather. Thinking back to the record snowfall of winter and the very wet spring, it was hard for people to realize that there was now a water shortage. Every drop became precious. After a miner had washed up at the end of his shift, his dirty bath water was distributed carefully around the vegetable garden. Dishes were washed once a day, and that water, too, went on the garden. Even the mine was almost dry, but the men liked that.

Then, at the end of July, influenza struck. The Piggotts first heard about it when their next door neighbour, Mr. Nicol, called to Mum over the back fence. He asked her to take a look at his wife. Mum persuaded him to call the doctor.

"Influenza," said Dr. Turner grimly. "She's the third case. We're in for it."

Everybody knew what he meant. There had been an influenza epidemic on the Island a year ago, and many people had died. Extension had escaped that time, but now the dread disease was here. Mum and Mrs. Gauthier arranged to care for the sick woman while her husband was at work. Millie was put in charge of Mrs. Nicol's chickens and ducks. These were the same birds she had spent so much time shooing over the fence in early spring when the fresh, new vegetable plants tempted them. Now she had to feed them and collect their eggs.

Soon nearly every house in Extension had at least one sick person.

One morning about ten o'clock, Millie and Ben came into the kitchen with the last of the crop of raspberries. Mum, who should have been scalding sealers to hold the preserved berries, was sitting at the table with her head in her right hand. She held out her left to ward off Ben as he darted towards her.

"What's wrong, Mummy? Are you sick?" he asked fearfully.

Millie felt as if an icy wind had blown over her. She set the pail on the table with care and stood with her hands pressing hard on the rim. Mum shook her head and spoke fretfully.

"I can't cope with the berries, Millie. I just can't. Get rid of them somehow."

Mum must be sick to talk like that! Millie thought. But she couldn't be! It was too awful to think about! She concentrated on the berries.

"I'll take them to the hotel," she said slowly. "Maybe the cook will buy them."

Mum didn't seem to notice her leaving.

The cook was glad to get the berries. He paid her ten cents and told her he'd buy any more she picked. On the way home, she still refused to think about sickness. Instead, she pictured the raspberry canes at the old house. She could make quite a bit money out of those. They might need it.

By the time Art came off shift, Mum was in bed. Millie had set up his bath outside. Afterwards, when he tried to lift the tub, he stumbled and spilled half the water.

"What are you doing?" screamed Millie. "We need that water!"

"Sorry," he said in a faint voice. "I don't feel so good." In spite of the heat, he was shivering. "I don't want to eat. I'm going to lie down."

At last, Millie had to admit the truth. Influenza had come to their house. She sent Ben in search of the doctor.

It was late evening before he could come. "They've both got it," he said. He ordered Art out of the stuffy loft and into the back bedroom. "Millie, you and the little fellow move into the front room," he said. "Now there's no medicine that will cure the 'flu. All you can do is nurse them carefully. When they're feverish, wipe them with cool cloths. If they're shivering, cover them up. And give them lots of liquids. Tea or plain water will do." He sighed. "You'll just have to do the best you can. I'll try to get you some help, but half the town's sick. Fortunately, no one has died yet, but they are having a very bad time for three or four days." He picked up his bag and walked to the front door. "Your mother's got a strong constitution. She'll pull through, but you must watch that boy." He scowled and his voice hardened. "I warned your parents long ago. He should never have gone underground. It's criminal with his lungs!"

Millie gave a squeak of fear. The doctor grunted.

"Ah, well, what's the use of railing at you, eh? Promise me you'll send for me the minute you think I'm needed."

"I will," whispered the frightened child.

The next three days were a nightmare. The doctor came back once. Mr. Nicol from next door kept the coal bucket and the water pail filled. One night another woman who lived on their street came in for a few hours so that Millie could sleep. It was frightening to see Mum so weak she couldn't sit up for more than five minutes at a time. It was worse to hear Art moaning and wheezing. Afterwards, Millie could never remember how she got through that time.

A week and a day after Mum took sick, Millie was sitting in the shade on the back step shelling peas. Life was back to normal. She and Ben were harvesting the vegetable crop; Mum and Art were both at work. Between them, they had lost seven days of wages. Their savings were almost wiped out.

Millie felt the tears rising up again as she remembered watching Art walk down the road with his lunch pail yesterday morning. He was never going to escape the mine. She had fled to the outhouse, the only place she could be alone. She'd locked the door and cried hard. Earlier, when she'd told Art and Mum what Dr. Turner had said, they had nearly snapped her head off.

"How does he expect us to live?" they demanded.

It isn't fair! thought Millie. I want to move away from the mine! It isn't fair!

She ripped open the next pod so violently that the peas scattered on the ground and were wasted. She stopped shelling and scowled. Something white moving in the back corner of the garden caught her eye.

Those ducks again! Trying to get into the garden! That was the last straw! She jumped up to chase them away, then saw Mr. Nicol hoeing his potato patch. She couldn't yell at his ducks. When Art and Mum were sick, he'd been very kind. He'd done a lot of heavy jobs for her, including fetching water from the well. She sat down and went on with her task. In her mind, though, she scolded the silly, white birds fiercely. Why were they always poking their heads through the fence? The vegetables were all well grown. Didn't they know there was nothing to eat? Stupid creatures!

Four of them were pressed against the

fence with their orange beaks bent down as though sniffing the earth. The place they were so anxious to reach was a bare patch of ground left uncultivated because it was so stony. There were two or three medium-sized rocks and lots of gravel. Two tufts of coarse, tall, green grass grew against the largest rock.

Ben brought her another basket of peas.

"That's all I can find," he said. "Can I go and play now?"

"Help me shell them, then you can go."

"Oh, Millie!"

"Here's a pot to put them in. Sit down and be quiet. I want to think."

He sat down beside her. "What about?"

"Ducks."

"Ducks! What for?"

"Well, look at that grass over there," Millie said. "How come it's green?"

Ben followed Millie's glance. Except for the trees whose roots reached deep into the earth and the garden plants which were watered so carefully, all the vegetation in town was withered and brown.

"Green grass means water," Millie said slowly. "And ducks are water birds." She put down the pan of peas and stood up.

"Hey! Where are you going?" asked Ben.

When Millie didn't answer, he followed her down to the corner of the lot. The ducks quacked and backed away. Millie stared at the ground. It was so dry that puffs of dust rose when Ben trod on it. Yet the ducks were attracted to it, and the grass was green.

"We need a shovel, Ben," she said, excited.

Ben didn't understand what for, but he ran to get one.

The earth was very hard, but Millie managed to dig down to the depth of the blade. The gravel on the tip of the tool was damp. Millie tried to dig some more.

"Look, Ben," Millie cried. "It's water!"

Puzzled, Ben stood and stared at the little hole. He was even more puzzled when his sister called to their neighbour.

"Mr. Nicol, can you come here?"

The man walked over and leaned on his hoe. He glanced to where Millie pointed, then bent over the fence for a closer look.

"What have you got here?" he asked.

Millie explained about the grass and the ducks.

"I thought there must be water and there is."

"By George!" said Mr. Nicol.

He dropped his hoe. In a minute he was

on their side of the fence. He took the spade from Millie.

"Stand back," he said.

The children watched the clods fly. Ben dodged the leaping shovel to peer into the hole.

"Water! Look, Millie, water!"

Laughing, the two children clasped hands and danced a jig behind the man's back.

"By George, lass, you've found a spring," said Mr. Nicol. "Fetch me some rocks."

Quickly, Millie and Ben brought him all they could find in the two gardens. The miner lined the bottom and the sides of the hole until he had made a miniature well. The three of them grinned as it slowly filled with water.

"Got an empty bucket, Ben?" asked the man.

When Ben brought it, Mr. Nicol dropped it into the makeshift well and brought it up half full. That emptied the hole, but more water seeped in slowly.

"This'll be a godsend to you," said Mr. Nicol. "I'll bet you get two pails a day from this."

"One is for you," Millie said quickly. "Your ducks showed us where it was, and you dug the hole."

"Well, thanks, we'll see how she pans o<
But think of a lass like you figuring out ther<
was a spring here! You're a wonder, you are!"
"Millie's great at finding things," Ben said
with pride.

Except, thought Millie, for the thing I most
want to find, Granddad's box. We really need
the money now.

I'll look for it tomorrow, she vowed to
herself. Maybe I'll be lucky two days in a row.

Chapter Eleven

*M*illie set out the next morning with two empty lard pails. She told Mum she was going to pick wild blackberries. Luckily, Mum thought the canes were too prickly for Ben so he stayed home. At the corner of her street, she met Amy.

"I'm going up to the old place to pick raspberries," Millie said. "Want to come?"

"You're crazy! Don't you remember what Bart Menzies said? It isn't safe!"

"I'm going," said Millie stubbornly.

"I'll walk up John Street with you," said Amy.

"If you want to," answered Millie.

They talked rather stiffly about Amy's visit to her cousins in Ladysmith until they were across the railway tracks. At the big rock on John Street, Amy said, "I came to say goodbye."

Startled, Millie asked, "Why? Where are you going?"

"Dad's got a new job in Cumberland. We're moving next week."

"Because your uncle's going there?"

Amy nodded.

Millie looked at her sideways. Her doubts must have shown in her face.

"They're about the only friends we have," Amy said bitterly.

Millie waited for her to say, "Except you," but she didn't. Had she been a friend to Amy? Lately, she had tried to be. She'd meant to try harder. She sighed inwardly. Good intentions didn't get a person very far.

"I'll be glad to get away from Frank," Amy said to break the silence.

Millie sighed aloud. "I can't see much difference between Extension and Cumberland," she said. "They're both coal towns. Everyone will know your Dad. They'll know you're his kid."

"But Prue will be in the same school!" said Amy gleefully.

Millie laughed. "She sure took care of Frank, didn't she?"

Amy stood still and made herself as tall as she could. "Hey, Cale," she said, pretending to be her cousin. "This kid thinks he's going to ruin the drill."

Instantly, Millie was Caleb. "This kid?" she asked in a deep voice. "Naw, he wouldn't do that. Not while I'm around."

The two girls giggled all the way to the end of the road.

Amy refused to step onto Ogden Street. Even Millie hesitated. The scene was much more desolate than it had been in June. The grasses were brown, the stems of the flowering plants stiff, and the leaves tiny. Insects buzzed angrily around withered blossoms.

"Everything looks dead," said Amy. "There won't be any berries."

"That's not really what I came for," answered Millie. "I'm going to get into our old house."

Amy gasped. "You can't! Mr. Menzies might be there."

"What if he is!"

She knew that Amy wouldn't go with her, but if she explained why she was going, Amy might wait for her. It would be a comfort to know she was nearby. But did she really want to share her secret hope? Before she could make up her mind, she heard a rumbling sound, like coal going down a chute, only muffled.

"What was that?" Amy whimpered.

She clutched Millie's arm as they looked toward the sound which seemed to come from the last house on the row.

"Oooh! Look!" gasped Amy.

Millie stared wide-eyed as the earth around the building cracked into fissures. Slowly, and almost without a sound, the house sank into the ground until all but the roof disappeared. Puffs of dust hung in the still air.

"A cave-in," breathed Millie, horrified.

Now the Piggott house tilted towards the hole. It broke along the seam line where it had been re-joined after its move. Over the crack of the snapping boards, they heard a man's voice yell. The top of the chimney collapsed with a clatter. Watching the rocks fall, Millie had a sudden, vivid vision of where Granddad had kept his box. It was in a hidey-hole behind one of the stones in the fireplace. She could see the small, dark hole. She could even hear the scrape of tin against cement as her mother pushed the box in, and the clink of stone against stone as she replaced the loose one. And now the house was sliding away!

Was her treasure going to end up in the abandoned mine shaft just when she'd found it?

Maybe not. The slide stopped. The two parts of the house remained upright with the front half more tilted than the back.

Amy turned towards town and pulled at Millie's skirt. "Let's go! Let's go! The whole street might fall in!"

Millie couldn't take her eyes off the ruins of her old home. Suddenly, she grabbed Amy's shoulders and forced her to look back at the house. A thin stream of smoke curled out of the break in the roof.

"Fire!" she screamed. "Amy, go for help! I'm going to find Mr. Menzies."

"You can't," Amy began, but she knew as well as Millie did the danger of fire in the tinder-dry area. This was not the time to stand and argue. She fled back down John Street screaming "Fire!" at the top of her lungs.

Millie heard her as she herself ran towards the house. She was sure it was the old miner who had yelled earlier. Was he inside the house or not?

There was no sign of him in the yard. Inside, then. The back step was still on level ground, but the scullery door sill was a very long step above it. She pulled herself up, crossed the room in three strides, and peered fearfully into the slanting kitchen.

Mr. Menzies lay on the floor with sections of stove pipe all around him. One of them had hit his forehead and raised a big, red lump. The stove was tilted, and the door of the fire box was hanging open. Coals had spilled out onto the floor. The smoke from one of these was what they had seen. At any moment the floor boards might burst into flame.

"Mr. Menzies," Millie called. "Wake up!"

She knelt beside him and shook his shoulder. He was breathing but didn't stir. If there was another cave-in, he'd slide right into the path of the fire. She couldn't waste time trying to wake him. She grabbed him under the arms and lugged him around so that she could drag him to the back door. He was heavy. Her arms ached. The scullery seemed twice as long as she remembered. At the open door, still holding him up, she paused for a rest. A low swoosh startled her. A tongue of flame ran across the floor toward the far wall. As she watched in horror, another ember ignited the wood. She must get out! How to get the unconscious man down to the ground? Her panic was interrupted by a voice yelling, "Hold it!"

A man reached past her, took the old man

by the waist, and swung him over his shoulder.

"Run fer it, girlie!" he ordered.

Millie fled to join a small group of women and children at the corner of John Street. The man deposited Mr. Menzies beside them and examined him quickly.

"He's alive," he said. "Take care of him."

Millie and two women bent over the old miner and called his name. One woman fanned him with her apron. In a minute he stirred and opened his eyes. He swore and struggled to a sitting position. Touching his head, he winced. He sniffed the air.

"Fire!" he said. He jumped up and took a step towards the house. Several hands grabbed him.

"No! You take it easy."

"There's enough men there now. It might cave again at any minute."

"Right you are," he said quietly. Then, "Who got me out?"

"She did," a woman answered, pointing at Millie.

He raised his eyebrows, then rested his hand on Millie's shoulder, and watched with her as the men worked.

Two men used shovels to dig a trench

around the building. One hacked away at the wall with an axe while another dragged the pieces away. Two more dumped buckets of earth on the flames to smother them.

The mine manager arrived with Amy at his heels. She went straight to Millie.

"Are you all right?" she asked.

"Yes, I'm fine. You're all out of puff."

"I ran all the way down to the office. And back."

"Sit down for a minute," Millie said. "It's going to be all right. See, the fire's out."

It was. Most of the men moved back to safety on the road. Mr. Warbell and the man who had helped Millie walked cautiously to the edge of the cave-in.

"He'll have to admit it now," growled Menzies. He sounded like his usual cranky self. "They never would admit they mined too close to the surface. How'll he explain this?"

"It'll have to be fenced off," a man agreed. "Should've been done years ago."

Fenced off! thought Millie. She'd never be allowed to look for Granddad's box! Just when she knew exactly where it was! Should she try to get it now? She looked at the men who were standing like guards around the area. They'd never let her through. And after she heard about the cave-in Mum would forbid her to come anywhere near here. Who would help her?

Everyone was looking towards Mr. Warbell. Those who knew the girls' story were telling it to others who had just arrived. Millie tugged Mr. Menzies's arm and pulled him apart from the group.

"What is it, girl?" he asked.

"I'm Millie Piggott. Hugh Piggott's grand-daughter."

"I know," the man answered. "I recognized you. I told you not to come back, but I'm glad you did."

"Mr. Menzies, I have to get into the house."

"Baloney! It's too dangerous!"

Quickly, Millie told him about Art and how they needed the money to get out of the mine. She told him about Granddad's box and explained exactly where it was. It wasn't a very clear story, but he seemed to understand.

"Please, Mr. Menzies, ask them to let me go and look."

The man shook his head. "No. It's too dangerous. I'll go myself. Oh-oh! Here's Warbell. Now there'll be a row!"

The argument was a humdinger. The mine

manager accused Bart Menzies of causing the fire by living in the house when he had been forbidden to be on Company property. Mr. Menzies roared about the lack of safety precautions by the Company. They both wore themselves out shouting.

"I'll just get my gear and be off," said Menzies.

"No one's to set foot on Ogden Street ever again!" yelled Mr. Warbell.

"For shame!" one woman said. "Let the poor man get his bits and pieces."

The manager looked around at the scowling faces. Millie held her breath. Did he care what these people thought?

Apparently, he did. "You've got five minutes," he growled. "And I'm timing you."

Mr. Menzies strode away.

Mr. Warbell talked to some of the men about getting a fence around the hole. The rest of the group watched the house in silence. Some of them sighed with relief when the old man jumped out of the back door. His arms were full of clothes, and a canvas bag dangled from one elbow.

"Get off home, all of you," ordered Mr. Warbell. "And you, Menzies, you old troublemaker, get out of town."

Millie and Amy walked besides Mr. Menzies. They lagged slightly behind the others.

"I notice you got no thanks from him," he said, "but I thank you both. If you hadn't been there—! But we won't think about that. You were both mighty level-headed."

Other people had already told them that. Compliments meant nothing to Millie at the moment.

"Did you get it?" she asked.

"Right where you said it was," he answered with a grin. "It's in the sack. Fish it out."

They stopped in the middle of the road. Millie reached into the canvas bag and her fingers touched metal. She drew out a small, rectangular tin box.

"What is it?" asked Amy.

"My granddad's savings," breathed Millie. She stared at the faces of the three pretty ladies on the battered lid. The yellow background paint was chipped in many places, but the red printing was still readable. Three Twins Fine Cut Smoking Tobacco. Remembering her grandfather, she smiled at Bart Menzies.

"Don't get yer hopes too high," he

warned. "There's plenty of times they could have emptied it."

Millie looked anxious. "But it's heavy," she said.

He shrugged. "Could be coppers."

"Open it," Amy said.

Millie flipped up the lid as she had often seen her grandfather do. There were a few coppers, but there were also many silver coins and some bills. She snapped the lid shut and hugged the box to her chest. She didn't know whether to laugh or cry.

"Looks like a good haul," Mr. Menzies said. "You'd better get it home to yer mother."

Millie laughed and jumped and tore away. "Bye," she called over her shoulder. "Thank you!"

Amy raced with her as far as the corner where they had met earlier.

Mum was in the kitchen when Millie burst in. She listened to the story in amazement, then plopped down at the table. Millie opened the box and dumped out the contents in front of her.

"Land sakes!" said Mum.

She sorted the coins and paper into piles as she counted.

"There's enough here for three months'

rent on the house in Ladysmith," she announced.

"Then we can do it, can't we?" demanded Millie. "We can get Art out of the mine!"

Mum made a sound between a laugh and a sob.

"We can, girl, and it's all thanks to you!"

Her mouth turned up in a smile, but there were tears in her eyes. Millie knew exactly how she felt.

When the whistle blew to end the shift at three-thirty, Ben met Art at the mine entrance so the older boy knew all about the box by the time he got home. He had to hold it in his hands before he could believe in it.

"Well, you were right, Millie. Beats me how you know where it was, though."

"I just pictured it in my mind," Millie answered.

Chapter Twelve

*A*rt decided to work until August 30th. His final wage packet would cover the rent they owed the Company and the cost of the move. On one of her days in town Mum arranged to rent the house in Ladysmith. She also talked to the boarders and persuaded them to stay on. Millie felt as though all her dreams had come true on the morning Art set off for his last shift.

His mother and sister promised him an extra special supper to celebrate. On Ben's advice, Mum made a chocolate layer cake with lots of icing. At three in the afternoon, she was spreading the icing on the cake while Ben noisily licked the bowl. Millie opened a jar of Art's favourite strawberry preserves and poured them into the pressed glass bowl they used only for very special occasions. As she set the bowl down in the middle of the table, the mine whistle blew.

"Sakes alive!" said Mum with a laugh. "That afternoon went fast!"

Millie looked at the kitchen clock. It read 3:16. Must be slow, she thought.

But the whistle went on blowing: past the signal for the end of the shift, past the call for the doctor, past the warning of an accident that had sounded when Dad died, and on up to the full six blasts to bring the rescue team to the scene of a major disaster.

All over the town women stood rigid and silent, counting the blasts, just as the Piggott women did.

When the whistle stopped, Effie moaned, "No! No! Please God! Not on his last shift!"

She dropped to her knees and bent her head over a chair seat. Frightened, Ben clung to his mother.

"I can't go, Millie," Effie said. "You go."

Millie didn't hear her. She felt as if she was in one of those nightmares in which you have to escape from some terrible danger but can't move. Suddenly she woke, stared wildly at her mother and Ben, then raced out the door.

Other white-faced women and children were hurrying to the pit head.

Millie arrived in time to see the rescue team going in amid a stream of miners coming out. All were grim-faced and silent. They had their names checked off, then joined the crowd around the entrance. In spite of the large number of miners from the day and evening shifts and the smaller number of townspeople, the air was eerily quiet. The coal cars no longer clattered in and out. The tipple shut down. The only sounds were the puffing of the train engine, the braying of some of the mules, and the low rumble of men's voices.

Rumours flew. It was a fire, an explosion, a cave-in; many dead, no one dead, three dead. There was one thing everyone agreed on: the trouble was on Level Two, Art's workplace.

He hadn't come out yet. Millie had searched among the men, and she knew that. Now she also knew that there had been an explosion. That meant gas. Those who escaped unhurt from the blast were in danger from the after-damp. The deadly methane gas would be blown throughout the Level by the force of the explosion.

Millie shivered. Just twenty minutes ago, she'd been so happy. She'd thought she had ended their troubles forever by finding Granddad's box of money. She'd thought Art was going to get out of the mine. Where was he now? Just when she felt she must scream with terror, her mother's arm wrapped her closely.

"I'm here," Effie whispered.

Millie burrowed into her mother's apron for a moment, then raised her head as a murmur ran through the crowd. She looked to the entrance. Out came a car carrying four men. All had scorched hands and faces. One was bleeding from a cut on his head, another cradled a broken arm.

"Any dead?" Mrs. Gauthier called, her voice full of fear.

"Not as far as I know," answered the man with the cut. Another car rattled out. Dick Shepherd was on it, supporting his badly-burned Dad.

Millie pushed her way forward and touched Dick's sleeve as some other men took his father from him.

"Art?" she croaked.

"Not hurt," he said quickly. "He's working the winch, to get them out faster."

He hurried away to catch up to his father. Millie went back and reported to Mum. They clung together in relief for a moment, but both knew they couldn't relax yet. Another explosion could happen any minute.

Why can't somebody else work the winch? thought Millie angrily. How come Dick is out here and Art's still down there in the dark? Dad would never have let a boy stay down there. Well, would he? She wasn't sure. After all, every miner is someone's brother or father or son.

As she continued to wait through each dragging minute, she thought more about Art. He was her brother and the most important person in the world to her, but he was also a miner with a responsibility to his fellow workers. Much as she loved him, she couldn't keep him safe forever. The move to Ladysmith wasn't going to be the end of all their trials and worries. It was only another town, not Fairyland. But, Oh, God, please, God, let them all be together there!

A long, shuddering sigh of relief rippled through the crowd. The rescue team emerged from the mine carrying three stretchers. Following them plodded three blackened, weary figures: Joe Rivers, the pit boss, Mr. Warbell, the mine manager, and between them, the young winch boy.

Millie's hands flew to cover her mouth. Tears filled her eyes.

Art walked straight into his mother's arms. Millie clung to one side of him and Ben the other. Millie couldn't tell whether it was she or Art who was trembling so violently.

After a moment, Art pushed away and spoke to the people standing nearby.

"They're all alive," he assured them. "I talked to them all."

Joe Rivers came up to Mum. "You've got a good man there, Mrs. Piggott. His Dad would have been proud of him. He stuck to his job to the very end. We'll miss him." He shook Art's hand. "Good luck in Ladysmith," he said.

The four Piggotts went home to a belated and subdued celebration. Even Ben found it impossible to be noisily happy. The narrow escape from tragedy was still too close. Nevertheless, they all grinned broadly over their lemonade when Mum proposed a toast.

"To our new life! Together!"